A SHADOW MOVED INTO THE BEDROOM. . . .

She waited a beat too long deciding whether to follow him out the window or backtrack to the glass door. She turned toward the door just as he came across the bed. He pulled her backward, flipping her under him as they landed hard on the bed.

"I like a woman who's active in bed, but you really push things to the limit," Logan said, imprisoning her wrists with his hands.

"Go to hell," Scottie said.

She didn't fight him but he didn't for a second believe she'd accepted defeat.

"You're just mad because I'm on top this time."

"Don't get used to it," she shot back.

He grinned. "Hey, I'm a sensitive guy. I let the woman be in control. Occasionally."

"Let?"

"What's the matter, Detective Princess, you don't like giving up control?" He pressed his lips close to her ear. "No matter what women say, they like being pulled beneath a nice hard body. . . ."

WHAT ARE *LOVESWEPT* ROMANCES?

They are stories of true romance and touching emotion. We believe those two very important ingredients are constants in our highly sensual and very believable stories in the LOVE-SWEPT line. Our goal is to give you, the reader, stories of consistently high quality that may sometimes make you laugh, sometimes make you cry, but are always fresh and creative and contain many delightful surprises within their pages.

Most romance fans read an enormous number of books. Those they truly love, they keep. Others may be traded with friends and soon forgotten. We hope that each LOVESWEPT romance will be a treasure—a "keeper." We will always try to publish

LOVE STORIES YOU'LL NEVER FORGET
BY AUTHORS YOU'LL ALWAYS REMEMBER

The Editors

882

DARK KNIGHT

DONNA KAUFFMAN

BANTAM BOOKS
NEW YORK · TORONTO · LONDON · SYDNEY · AUCKLAND

DARK KNIGHT

A Bantam Book / April 1998

ISBN 0-553-44578-2

Published simultaneously in the United States and Canada

Bantam Books are published by Bantam Books, a division of Bantam Dou-
bleday Dell Publishing Group, Inc. Its trademark, consisting of the words
"Bantam Books" and the portrayal of a rooster, is Registered in U.S.
Patent and Trademark Office and in other countries. Marca Registrada.
Bantam Books, 1540 Broadway, New York, New York 10036.

PRINTED IN THE UNITED STATES OF AMERICA

OPM   10 9 8 7 6 5 4 3 2 1

This book is dedicated to my favorite bookseller and number one author promoter, Jan Robison.

For your unfailing support and words of encouragement, you have my eternal appreciation.

I wish there were more like you.

ONE

In the end, it was the Grinch that made her cry.

"This is ridiculous." Scottie Giardi punched the off button on the remote, tossed her wadded-up tissue on the coffee table, and dragged herself off the couch. She wandered over to the glass doors that led to her tenth-floor balcony and watched the large, wet snowflakes drifting relentlessly downward, blanketing the downtown streets and buildings, promising that tomorrow morning the children of Denver would waken to a white Christmas. Soundless and glittering with light, the city looked even more magical than Dr. Seuss's *Who*-ville.

She leaned her aching forehead against the glass. "Bah humbug." But the catch in her voice gave her true feelings away.

She closed her eyes. The steady beat of her pulse clicked away in her head like an alarm clock, each beat the same, giving no clue as to which tick would be the last one. Then BOOM! One day the bell would ring, and it would be too late.

Too late for friendships. Too late for love. Too late for children. Too damn late.

She turned away and stalked to the bathroom. She didn't want love. She didn't need friendships. And she had long ago come to terms with the fact that she would never have children. A hot shower and a cold drink would loosen the tension that had been plaguing her all evening.

As head of a secret government task force, known privately as Delgado's Dirty Dozen, she was always on call, but they were in the final phases of rebuilding and restructuring the team. The few assignments they were currently handling were all running smoothly.

There was very little chance anyone would need her tonight. The thought made her eyes suddenly burn. She blinked hard several times and yanked on the shower.

The steaming spray beat down on her head, pounded into her shoulders, ran over her face. She tried to relax, but it felt as if every muscle she had was an individual knot. *What in the hell is wrong with you, Giardi?*

If she hadn't felt so much like crying, she would have laughed. How many times had she heard those exact words?

The voice that echoed loudest in her mind was her father's. Followed closely by her late husband, Jim's. A humorless smile trembled on her lips. No doubt they'd both be amused to know their harsh indictments haunted her in death every bit as much as they'd haunted her when both men had been alive.

She abruptly shut off the shower, snagged a towel, and rubbed her body with brisk strokes. She knew better than to think she could rub away the memories as easily as she could the water droplets, just as she knew she'd keep trying anyway. Especially tonight.

Eleven years. It had been exactly eleven years since her father and Jim had been shot in the line of duty, and she'd yet to feel remorse. Guilt? Yes. Self-recrimination? Boatloads of it. Relief . . . Oh yes. So much so, she still felt the rush of it now, all these many years and miles later. Which circled her right back to the guilt.

She pulled on a Washington Redskins jersey, then headed for the kitchen. Sipping a glass of chilled zinfandel, she avoided looking toward the balcony doors and flipped on the TV. CNN was always good for a distraction. She hated admitting she needed one.

If she couldn't escape to some faraway place where they'd never heard of snow, much less Christmas, she could watch it and wish she were there. But instead of finding sanctuary with some hard-edged reporter spouting gritty details of this week's current country in crisis, Cindy-Lou Who blazed onto the screen, looking up at the Grinch with her wide, innocent eyes. Scottie went to stab at the channel button, but somehow her fingers wouldn't move. And the screen was all blurry. It took several seconds for her to realize she was crying.

Anger didn't come to her rescue this time, nor did self-disgust. There was no escape. God knew she'd tried them all.

For the first time in ten years, since she'd left the Metropolitan police force in Washington, D.C., and taken Seve "Del" Delgado up on his lifesaving offer of a place on his special forces team, she had no convenient corner of the globe to run to. Earlier this year, Del had been forced to reveal his background during testimony in a mob trial. For his safety and that of the team, he'd received a new identity, a new face, and had left the team in her hands, never to be heard from again.

Only now did she realize it hadn't been ten years of freedom, but ten years of escape.

The sudden jangle of the phone made her jump. She swore at herself, then went on full alert as it registered that it was her private office line ringing. *Bless you.* She moved swiftly to the small office next to her bedroom, shamelessly not caring what emergency awaited on the other end of the line.

With utter relief, she let her mind slip back to her job, dismissing the hours of painful introspection as if they'd never existed. Safe once again in the sanctuary of her work.

She lifted the phone to her ear and waited for the current code to be recited. The code came. It was the voice that delivered it that stunned her into complete silence.

"Giardi, I know it's a shock to hear my voice, but I'm short on time. I'll explain later."

"Del?" Her voice was a stunned whisper.

"*Sí,*" he responded in his usual clipped tones. "Now listen closely. We have a problem."

"We?" Scottie straightened, her mind focusing quickly as the initial shock wore off. "*We* have a problem?" Her tone was just as abrupt. She'd learned more than espionage tactics from the man on the other end of the line.

A short pause followed. "Yes, we."

Scottie had often speculated that Del was still somehow involved with the team. She'd always had a niggling sensation that he was hovering somewhere, keeping an eye on her and his precious Dirty Dozen. What was left of them anyway. The fact that he had the code, a new one she'd just put into the system earlier that evening before finally making herself leave the office, proved he was doing a lot more than hovering—and from an inside position.

"Pack for Code Yellow, there will be a private transport waiting for you at the airfield on tarmac three."

Scottie didn't question the feasibility of flying out of Denver given the current weather system. If Del had a plane on standby, then it could fly her out. "Destination?"

"Montana."

Their caseload was minimal at the moment. They had only three assignments running. One of them was in Montana. Lucas Blackstone was heading it. He was the last original team member still in the field. She stifled the swift pang of envy.

"Situation?" she asked.

"We don't have a code for this one."

That got her attention. "Excuse me?"

"Seems Blackstone has a brother. The brother has been searching for him and somehow managed to track him all the way to Montana."

"To the Brethren? How did this guy find him? Not from Lucas."

"That's what we want to find out. And no, to our knowledge Lucas has no idea of this guy's existence."

That part didn't surprise her, but she breathed a sigh of relief. One of the mandatory qualifications for becoming a Dirty Dozen team member was that one have no family, no friends. Invulnerable. "Who fell down on the job then? Why the hell didn't someone notify me?

We could have had the brother picked up before he ever got so close."

"Well, we didn't know what was going on at first."

"There's that *we* again. Del, I'm thrilled to hear your voice, but I'm not real happy here."

"There's no time to go into that now. The reason we didn't pick him up right away was because we didn't know it was his brother. We thought it was Lucas."

Scottie rubbed her temple. "What?"

"Lucas Blackstone has a twin brother. As in identical twin." He didn't wait for her reaction. "Name is Logan Blackstone. He's a slippery *hombre*. Way too smart for his good or ours. You know we're in the critical stages of this mission."

"Apparently there's a lot I *don't* know," she said. "I didn't realize my job came with marionette strings, Del."

He let loose a string of invectives, all in his native Spanish. She fought a sudden smile. She probably wouldn't recognize him now if she bumped into him in broad daylight, but there was no doubting he was Seve Delgado.

"You'll get no apologies from me on this, Giardi. You will get an explanation. But not now. This Brethren thing is going to blow wide by New Year's Eve. Blackstone sent word out that the cult leaders are planning a Jonestown at the stroke of midnight."

Scottie's anger and irritation fled. "But we thought—"

"We thought wrong. The drugs they've been smuggling down across the border from Canada aren't for distribution. They're for—"

"Self-destruction."

Del didn't have to confirm. "Normally, I'd say let the crazy bastards kill themselves, including Senator Gladiston's idiot daughter. But we have an official count of sixteen children. Most under age seven."

"Oh, Del."

"*Sí.* We have to get them out. Our original cover of rescuing the good senator's daughter still gives us the perfect in. If all goes right, we can make everyone happy. I want you to get to Logan and do whatever you have to to keep him the hell out of the way until Lucas wraps this up. If any of the Brethren sight Logan and mistake him for Lucas . . ." He didn't have to spell out the implications of having a look-alike blunder unknowingly into such a delicate situation.

"Does Senator Gladiston know about this yet?"

"No. And I plan on keeping it that way. It's bad enough I have to deal with the DEA on this." His tone made it clear she wasn't the only one upset by how the whole thing had been handled. "There will be a full brief waiting for you in the plane. There isn't much to brief you on. Sorry."

Sorry? She could kiss the man. He'd given her the perfect Christmas present: no Christmas. "No apologies. You just saved my life." Again.

"Giardi?"

She heard the bare trace of concern in his voice and felt her throat tighten. Del was the closest thing to a real father she'd ever had. Not that she'd ever told him. And now was not the time either. "I can be on the field in fifteen minutes."

"I'll let them know. I appreciate this, Scottie." If there was something more than brisk efficiency in his tone, neither of them commented on it. "You'll have questions for me. I'll arrange a meeting when you're done with this assignment."

"I'm counting on it. Who'll mind the store while I'm away?"

"It'll be taken care of."

She paused briefly. Despite her relief at this unexpected reprieve, having her authority usurped so easily, even if it was by the man who had bestowed it on her in the first place, didn't sit well with her. "You'd better schedule a long meeting, Del."

She thought she actually heard him chuckle. Must have been static on the line. "Handle this one," he said. "I'll answer all your questions after."

"Yes, you will," she replied, but the line was already dead.

The small jet touched down in Montana on the landing strip under a clear sky and a full moon. It was just past midnight. "Merry Christmas to me," Scottie murmured, then turned back to the tiny glowing screen of her specially designed Personal Digital Assistant. Del hadn't been kidding about the brevity of the report. She knew little more now than when Del had disconnected their call.

She knew that Logan Blackstone was indeed Lucas's identical twin. They had apparently been separated by their never-married parents shortly after their birth, the father taking Logan, the mother taking Lucas. Both children were raised with the name Blackstone, each believing the other parent had died, and with no knowledge they had a sibling, much less an identical twin.

The team already had documentation that Lucas's

mother died when he was four. No family member had stepped forward as guardian, so Lucas had been raised in the foster care system. He'd entered the military at age eighteen and had eventually become a Green Beret. A loner, he'd never married, had few friends outside the other Berets. He'd gone on to do Special Forces work until Del had recruited him ten years earlier at age twenty-seven. The documentation of his birth and his mother's background hadn't revealed the existence of any living relatives. They had been sufficiently assured that Lucas Blackstone was a viable recruit for the team. But Scottie knew all this. She'd read Lucas's file when she'd taken on the job of directing the team.

There was no information on how Logan had discovered Lucas's existence, but there was documentation that their father had passed away two months earlier. Had he made a deathbed confession perhaps?

However Logan had discovered the information, the fact remained that he had made it his mission in life to track down his twin brother. And for a former Detroit street cop who'd spent the last five years as co-owner and operator of his late father's pub—his father also having been a retired cop—he'd been remarkably successful. Not to mention disturbingly resourceful.

A cop. A second-generation cop. Just like her. Just what she didn't need. Scottie sighed in disgust as she programmed the handheld machine to encrypt the information. She stood and stretched as best she could in the small confines of the jet cabin, then snagged her backpack, shoved the PDA into an inner pocket, and zipped it up tight.

The report didn't tell her the one thing she wanted

to know: How in the hell had a cop-turned-bartender managed to get so close?

"All clear, Ms. Giardi." The pilot turned in his seat. "Just got a message that your vehicle is waiting for you about fifty yards straight out. Report's in the usual place." He stood, opened the hatch, and lowered the steps.

"Thanks, Tom." She tugged her pack over her shoulder, balancing the weight on her back. "You heading back tonight?"

"Yep, gotta beat Santa home."

She ignored the odd pang his words elicited inside her chest. "I appreciate your taking the flight tonight." She wondered briefly who'd made the call. Who else knew Del had resurfaced?

"No problem, Ms. Giardi. Anytime."

Scottie heard him taxi around as she crossed the small field. She turned and watched Tom take off, unable to keep from wondering what it must be like to know someone was waiting for your arrival with open arms and a smile. Her laugh was derisive as she turned back to the black Land Rover, tossed her bag to the ground, and flung her arms wide. "Hi honey, I'm home."

Her smile faded as she ran a quick visual scan of the area before punching in the code to unlock the doors. Pine Lodge, Montana, gave the word "remote" an entirely new meaning. There was no warning prickling sensation tingling her scalp. Whoever had left the truck, and it was likely it had been one of Del's men, since she didn't have anyone in place there with the connections to pull it off, was long gone. She was alone.

She finally allowed herself to acknowledge the low

hum of adrenaline that had steadily pumped through her system since the instant the phone had rung. It felt good, she realized. Damn good. God, she had missed being out in the field.

Man, you are losing it, Giardi. You spend the evening sniveling like a whiny yuppie because your eggs are jumping around a bit, and now you're all mopey because you aren't playing Jane Bond anymore. She smiled. "What in the hell *is* wrong with you, Giardi?"

She slid into the driver's seat, reached under it, and felt around, then depressed a small panel. A tiny diskette slid into her palm, which she tucked into a hidden slot in the side of her PDA. Directions to a rental unit Logan had signed for three days earlier flashed on the tiny screen. He was in a cabin up on the north ridge of the Crazies, a small mountain range less than an hour from the Brethren compound. According to the rest of the information, a high-elevation snowfall had trapped him up there. But the snow was melting off. And Del's other men were needed at the compound. She had to get to Logan before he got off that mountain.

"Sounds like a fun vacation," she muttered. *Hey, it beats an evening with Cindy-Lou and the Whos.* Not wanting to think about where her head had been several hours before, she switched off the PDA and pocketed it, then put the disc in the dashboard ashtray and closed it. She heard the crunch, signifying the tiny compactor had done its job and demolished the disc. She smiled with satisfaction and shifted gears.

"Ready or not, Logan Blackstone, here I come."

❖━━━❖

Five hours and considerable exhaustion later, Scottie eased into a crouch behind a large pile of stones. The cabin was about fifty yards dead ahead. Obviously built for use by hunters, it was nestled in a clearing on the leeward side of a fairly steep rise. A steady stream of smoke trailed from the single chimney. She sniffed the air. Woodstove. There were no lights on inside and no sign of activity, no tracks outside.

A green truck, up to its oversize tires in snow, was parked in front. A white lump that was the snowmobile was situated out back.

She thought about the snowmobile she'd hidden a mile back down the mountain. A shame their design team hadn't been able to figure out a way to make those things silent. She was tired and half dead from the two-hour climb up the last section of the mountain. She hoped Mr. Blackstone didn't mind if she put him out of commission long enough for her to take a hot shower and a brief nap.

Del hadn't left any instructions on exactly how he expected her to contain Logan Blackstone, other than that simple surveillance would not be enough. Which meant there was only one way to handle this: Take prisoners, apologize later.

She stowed her pack behind the boulders, then ran along the tree line in a half crouch before darting into the truck. She worked quickly to disable it, then moved back around to the snowmobile and did the same there. She checked the house. Still quiet. No lights, no sounds.

"Sleeping like a baby. Let's see if I can extend your stay in dreamland a bit." She patted the zippered pocket of her parka and felt the leather case. All set.

She headed quietly to the back corner of the cabin.

Del's team had been thorough. The bedroom window was on the far side of the cabin. She was currently beneath the kitchen window. There was no security system, so it was a no-brainer B & E. Still, she didn't take any unnecessary chances. Just by being there Logan had proved he was not to be underestimated.

She quietly jimmied the sliding glass door, then slipped inside. She was standing in the open space between the kitchen and the living area. Furnishings were sparse and utilitarian. She guessed hunters didn't care much for decor, only a place to eat and sleep between killing things.

She removed her parka and slipped the leather case from the pocket before moving silently toward the door leading to the only bedroom. It surprised her that whoever had built the place had seen a need for interior walls at all. She peeked around the corner . . . and froze.

She had no idea what she'd expected, but it hadn't been the naked man sprawled on his back across the double bed.

He was big and dark, with skin that looked tawny even in the predawn light, skin that was wrapped tightly over sinewy muscles. He looked . . . primitive. Like a jungle predator at rest. The bed was framed with thick poles of rough-hewn oak. It barely contained him. The white linen sheet was twisted around him as if he'd been wrestling alligators in his sleep. The blankets and pillows were flung on the floor, previous victims who'd already lost their battles.

He grumbled something, then wrenched onto his stomach as if some invisible force had shoved him. Her mouth went dry. A coil of white linen between his legs was all that covered him. Somewhere she found enough spit to swallow. But she couldn't dredge up a denial. She wanted that sheet gone. In fact, she curled her hands into fists against the temptation to step into the room, grab the sheet, and tug it the rest of the way off of him.

The man was simply too glorious to be covered. He deserved to be naked. He had the kind of sprawled grace that would make artists of any medium salivate.

"Sarah." The rasp of a name sounded as if it had been dragged over hot coals before escaping from his lips.

All thoughts of artistic appreciation fled. She watched, a visual captive, as he clawed the sides of the mattress, the muscles in his shoulders and back bunching under the intensity of his grip. She could hear a pulsing sound and only absently acknowledged it was her own heartbeat thrumming in her ears.

Then he began to move. Writhe was the word that came to mind. His hips lifted slightly, then pressed deeply into the bed. He groaned in his sleep, turning his head from side to side, a tumble of black hair obscuring his face. He dug his knees and toes into the mattress, then ground his hips down again; the sounds he made were a tumble of dark, guttural need mixed with anguish. "Sarah . . . no. Don't! Need . . . you."

Scottie felt her nipples tighten in automatic reaction and found herself wondering who in the hell Sarah was . . . and why she was jealous of a woman she'd never met.

She strangled her libido, which had chosen a highly inconvenient time to come out of hibernation, then quickly unzipped the small leather case. He thrashed again, moaned something unintelligible, then quieted once more—except for his hips, which slid again and again along the smooth white sheet. Scottie forced herself to concentrate on prepping the syringe. It took a considerable amount of self-control.

The task complete, she depressed the plunger until the contents beaded at the end of the needle, then turned to her quarry. Good Lord but the man was a beautiful creature. She stepped closer to the bed, thinking it was almost a shame she was going to have to dress him later.

She moved the last step, then stopped dead when he suddenly twisted onto his back. His chest was sheened with sweat now, rising and falling rapidly. She darted her gaze to his face. Still dreaming.

"Sarah," he said with a groan, then reached down and tugged at the sheet between his legs.

Scottie gripped the syringe so hard, she was surprised she didn't snap the casing. She bent over and aimed the needle at the hard curve of his buttocks. "Sorry I can't let you finish this," she said under her breath, "but I have my orders." There was no escaping watching his continued motions. "Really sorry," she added silently.

He arched up and yanked hard, a low growl ripped from his throat. The sheet whipped off the bed like a white lash.

She pulled back just in time, then froze. He was gloriously naked . . . and gloriously erect. Her gaze was riveted to him as his thighs relaxed, then flexed again. His neatly carved abdominal muscles rippled like a wave as he hunched forward. Nothing short of sudden death could have stopped her from watching him. It was an elegant, erotic ballet of sinew and muscle, control and leashed power. Her hand shook slightly, and she had to lock her knees against the shockingly sudden hot clench of need that gripped the muscles between her thighs in a painful fist.

Then, without warning, his eyes flew open and locked on hers. In one lightning-quick motion his hand flashed out, grabbed her arm, and yanked her down.

Caught badly off balance and even more off guard, Scottie pitched forward. She landed hard across his chest and legs, barely managing to swing the hand with the syringe wide. She held on to it, even when he neatly flipped her onto her back and pinned her legs and arms to the bed.

He raised over her like a dark specter, monstrous and all-powerful. "Who the hell are you?" he demanded roughly.

TWO

Scottie masked her surprise and her anger at being so neatly maneuvered. She wasted a second wondering if he'd been asleep at all, or if it had been an elaborate display to distract her. If so, it had worked. Too damn well.

Keeping her gaze locked with his, she spoke evenly, wanting to keep his attention on her eyes, not the needle in her hand. "I'm here to save your ass."

His dark gaze didn't so much as flicker from hers. "I wasn't aware it required preserving." The rough texture of sleep faded from his voice, leaving it silky, soft, and far more dangerous. "You have a strange way of showing your . . . appreciation."

The pause was perfectly timed, the words delivered with seductive perfection. She knew that, understood it, yet the knowledge did nothing to prevent her body's instant reaction. He was good. No. He was better than good. He was lethal.

She should be focusing exclusively on her goal: rendering him inactive. Instead, she was excruciatingly aware of his nakedness, of the weight of his body on hers, of exactly what parts of him pressed against her . . . and where. She studied his face, looking for any sign that he could read her thoughts. Nothing. He was expressionless. She wished she were half as good.

"Drop the syringe," he said. The demand was delivered almost negligently. It was his autocratic confidence that finally gave her the mental foothold she needed to get her edge back.

She had one possible ace. She played it. "Who's Sarah?"

Jackpot. His mask faltered, and for one instant his grip on her wrists loosened. It was all the opening she needed. She yanked him closer. There was a flash of surprise in his eyes as he pitched forward, then her training clicked in and she saw nothing but motion. She felt him tense, coil, and knew she had only mere seconds to complete her task. Someone had trained him extremely well. *Admire his technique later, Giardi.*

He pulled on her to lever himself forward . . . but it was too late. She slammed her hand down and found her target; the nice hard flesh of his thigh. Not her original target, but effective enough.

He swiped at the needle and missed. She pushed in the plunger, then yanked the needle free and tossed the spent syringe across the room. His head reared up, his eyes glittered fiercely as his hand moved to her throat with deadly precision. "Son of a—" His eyes rolled upward before he could complete the expletive.

"Say good night, Blackstone." She shifted before he collapsed directly on top of her.

Breathing heavily, she dragged his arm and leg off of

her and crawled off the bed. She allowed herself a full minute to get her pulse rate back down, but that was all the luxury she could afford. The drug she'd pumped into him would keep most men his size out for at least fifteen to twenty minutes. Judging from their brief acquaintance, she gave him ten, max.

She quickly sorted through several options. She had the means to put him out of commission for a long period of time, but drugging people wasn't something she did lightly. She'd never been comfortable with that method. Not only was it dangerous, no matter how carefully administered, but to her it had always seemed the fool's way out.

She studied Blackstone and actually had second thoughts. Still, Logan Blackstone had revealed himself to be a surprisingly viable force of one. No police department trained their men that well. He would challenge her to the extreme of her abilities. She couldn't decide if she was more intrigued or annoyed.

"No more drugs." She pushed up the sleeve of her black thermal turtleneck and pressed the button on the side of her watch. Eight minutes. She slipped swiftly back outside and retrieved her backpack, pulling out the equipment she needed by touch as she moved quickly inside again. She dropped the backpack on the table, then scooped up the necessary gear. A wristwatch check showed she had five minutes remaining. The sun was close to the horizon, filling the cabin with a dull pink glow.

He was as she left him. Even prepared, the sight of him gave her an instant's pause. What the hell, she decided, as she knelt and checked the bedframe for sturdiness, she might as well enjoy the view. Her job came with few enough perks. Once he was conscious, she doubted she'd have time to indulge in anything remotely self-serving.

The metal mattress rack bracketed by the huge oak frame was solid iron. Perfect. She swiftly attached the clamps to the iron frame at both the foot and head of the bed, then stood and calculated her next move. He had to go on his back. There was no other way. She sighed, then moved to the opposite side of the bed. She pressed two fingers to his neck. His pulse was slow and steady. Maybe she'd get a few more minutes after all. He hadn't stirred an inch. She knelt on the bed and anchored an arm under his shoulder, then reached across him and gripped his other forearm. With one tug, she moved him silently to his back. Not so much as an exhale escaped his lips.

Why was she looking at his lips? She scowled, even as she grudgingly admired his control. Damn, but the man was self-controlled even in unconsciousness. His face was all angular planes, with a wide forehead and a square chin blocking out the rest of the shape. He had no noticeable scars, but his nose had been rearranged once or twice. And yet, his wider than average mouth somehow managed to create the perfect contrast. Despite the godlike physique, he wasn't handsome. The image of his dark eyes flashing fire popped into her head. No, handsome did not describe Logan Blackstone. Primal. Feral. Dangerous. Hunter. Those were the words that came to mind.

So, why was she staring at him as if she were a mesmerized teenager instead of caging the beast?

Muttering under her breath, she looked away and pulled the straps across the bed. It took several precious minutes to fasten the restraint onto his wrists, which were now crossed over his chest. She checked their security. Satisfied, she slid to the foot of the bed, tugged his lower torso over, and rearranged his legs while never looking higher than his calves. They were all angular planes too. She recalled his abdomen had been a carved monument to perfectly sculpted muscles, and then there was his . . .

She shut her mind down and yanked the straps up. She had one around his ankle when it occurred to her she should have at least found him some shorts. Balancing on her heels, she ran a scan around the room, but only saw sheets and pillows in a tangled heap. The man had to own some clothes. There was no closet in the room, just an old armoire with the doors missing and a ratty cane chair. Both were empty. She ducked down. Aha. A military-green duffel was under the bed.

"Is that where you learned to fight like a jungle cat, Blackstone?" she said under her breath. Del's report hadn't said anything about a stint in any branch of the service, and Del was nothing if not thorough, even on limited time. A military record would have popped up on the first go-around.

Her mind spun back to Del's sudden reappearance as she stretched for the duffel handle, when a low groan made her freeze. She stayed still less than a heartbeat, rolling to her knees and moving immediately for the ankle straps.

"You lose, Blackstone. Naked it is."

As it was, she barely got the second ankle wing secure before he started to wake. She managed to stand and snag a sheet from the floor. His eyes opened just as the white linen drifted down over his waist and thighs.

He located her immediately, but didn't move or say anything. Lethal. The word flitted through her mind again as she held his unwavering, surprisingly clear stare.

Time spun out, a minute and then two. Not wanting to admit—or reveal—that he was actually unnerving her, she purposely broke their visual standoff with a casual glance at her wristwatch. "Eleven minutes. Not bad."

He remained expressionless. It was a rare human who could come to consciousness to find himself being held hostage by a stranger, bound and trussed—not to mention naked—and not automatically test his restraints and demand explanations.

Logan Blackstone was a rare human indeed. The only thing he'd moved so far were his eyelids. She found she was the one wanting to demand explanations. *Just who are you, Logan Blackstone?*

She knew one thing, he was definitely Lucas's twin. No plastic surgeon, not even one of theirs, could have rendered such a close approximation. The facial similarities were uncanny for two men who'd spent a lifetime apart. The only stark difference being Logan's broken nose. Lucas had suffered his own bumps and fractures during the course of his career, but his had healed differently.

No, a plastic surgeon wouldn't have made that big of a mistake. Logan Blackstone was the real McCoy. His body was bigger, more heavily muscled than Lucas's lean, whipcord frame. Of course, she'd never seen Lucas stark naked, nor had she felt the weight of him pinning her down—

"Enjoying the show?" His dark voice snagged her attention. She had been staring.

"Admiring my handiwork." Her tone was cool. The rest of her was anything but.

His gaze swept slowly over her, his manner thorough, calculated—and not the least bit sexual. She refused to examine why that frustrated her.

"I'm not a real fan of bondage," he said. He'd yet to move a fraction. The subtle amusement in his tone was not reflected on his face or in his eyes. Both were completely expressionless. "I *am* choosy about my partners, but if you were this determined to have me, I imagine we could have come to a less . . . extreme agreement."

"If that was what I was after, Mr. Blackstone, I assure you I wouldn't have had to tie you up."

A brief light flashed in his eyes. Admiration? Doubtful. But there had been a reaction. It was a start.

"So, you aren't into kinky sex and you know my name. I don't suppose you'd care to tell me who you are? Or what you meant by saving my ass? I mean, isn't being shackled naked to my own bed enough of a disadvantage?"

Smooth, sexy aplomb. It was hard to imagine that satin-sheet voice making as rough a demand as he had earlier.

Just how badly was it bothering him to have lost control earlier? Was he angry somewhere far behind those cool, empty eyes?

Scottie tamped down her irritation before he detected it. Her function was to contain, then maintain. No less, but no more. Yet there was no denying he intrigued her. He was too perfectly controlled to ignore.

She was fully aware that engaging one's captor in

any sort of interplay was a survival tactic meant to buy time and search for weaknesses. She intended to show him she had none.

Purposely remaining silent, she stepped closer and checked the restraints at his ankles. She felt his gaze on hers, but he didn't so much as flinch as she tugged the black nylon straps. She moved to the head of the bed and bent close, irritated further that she was too uncertain of her ability to remain expressionless to look him casually in the eyes.

She was close enough to feel his breath fan her neck, to sense the heat of his skin. She was careful to remain at an angle that prevented him from suddenly lunging his head forward in an effort to crack her chin or cheekbone. He didn't try to watch what she was doing. His gaze was a hot, almost tangible thing, and it stayed locked on her face. She didn't question how she knew this, neither did she look for proof.

She kept her motions swift and efficient as she checked the straps. She went out of her way to touch only the nylon. She was certain he knew that.

"You didn't need to check them. You've done this before."

His unexpected speech froze her, but only momentarily.

When she stepped back and finally allowed herself to meet his eyes, the shade of amusement she heard in his voice was not reflected in their dark depths. She had no idea what he was really feeling. Instinct told her that beneath his smooth exterior, he was seething. He didn't reveal even a trace of anger, but she knew she was right. It was exactly how she would have felt.

Her gaze drifted over his thick neck and wide shoulders, across the breadth of his chest. She watched his smooth-skinned pectorals rise and fall, the way the motion pressed at his biceps, all bunched up due to the way he was restrained. A small, shaky breath escaped her lips. How would she fare if the tables were turned?

She hoped to hell she never had to find out.

She strode from the room, fingers itching to grab the doorknob and swing hard. She resisted. Despite the fact that he was restrained, she still could not afford the tiniest slipup.

"I like my eggs fried," he called out. "No bacon. A little juice if you have it. Freshly squeezed."

She resisted the urge to turn around. She had less success containing the sudden urge to smile. Damn, but the man did have style. Under other circumstances, she'd think about possibly recruiting him.

"Black coffee," he continued. "Precinct style."

Scottie's stride slipped imperceptibly.

"That's right, princess," he said. "You got cop written all over you. From your no-nonsense face right down to your hard little ass."

She pulled her pack across the dining room table. He was far too observant.

"Lieutenant Princess?"

She yanked open a zipper.

"Okay," he said, amusement once again in his voice. "Not a lieutenant. Let's try . . . gold shield. Detective."

How was it that he was the one strapped naked to the bed, yet she was the one who felt exposed? She dug around, pushing past her supply of power bars until her hand hit upon her secret stash. She yanked the candy bar out and tore off the brown wrapper. Chocolate, the true source of power in the universe.

"Big city. Not Detroit. Not New York. No accent. I'd rule out Chicago and Philly too. Miami. That's a possibility."

She took a small breath to settle her nerves. He was the hostage, she reminded herself. Let him ramble. It was a harmless enough diversion.

Or it should have been. He was good. She found herself wondering what had made him leave the force. She bet he'd made a great cop.

"Dallas. Nah. L.A. Nope."

An obnoxiously great cop.

Some small demon inside her made her turn so she was in full view of him before she unrepentantly bit off a chunk of gooey chocolate.

"Ouch. I think that actually hurt."

She didn't smile, though she wanted to. Annoyance made her lean her weight against the table and slowly finish off the candy bar, making sure the stringy pieces of caramel were visible with each bite. It was highly unprofessional behavior, but temporarily gratifying. Logan Blackstone could provoke a saint. She was no saint.

The man she'd woken up was a raging beast. She knew exactly how to contain that threat and had. She crumpled up the wrapper.

"Didn't your mama ever tell you it was impolite not to share?" he said.

"I never had a mama." She'd had no intention of replying. It had slipped out.

"That explains a lot of things."

It killed her not to ask him to explain and, damn the man, she knew he knew it.

"Well, if you're a Daddy's girl, then Daddy must have been a cop too."

She straightened away from the table and tossed the balled-up wrapper at the trashcan. Her shot was perfect. Her control was not. "You like playing guessing games, Blackstone?"

There was a pause. "I prefer to call it deductive reasoning based on acute awareness of my surroundings and close observation of the people who pass in and out of it."

He was entirely too smooth. His pause had been designed to make sure she knew he'd scored a point in getting her to talk at all. She faced him across the growing closeness of the cabin.

"Well then, deduce this. You can play games all you want, but it won't change one fundamental fact. Because of circumstances beyond your immediate control, you and I will be keeping company for a few days. I will gladly explain all I can once this is over, but until then, I can't give you any information or answer any of your questions. It is not my intention to hurt you."

His expression didn't change, but there seemed an almost palpable surge of energy emanating from him. She could feel it vibrating in the air. She deflected it with words. "However, if it makes my life easier, I do have means to make your temporary incarceration a more . . . restful one." She strode to the door. "Which will it be, Blackstone?"

His face was absolutely devoid of emotion.

"No more needles." His voice was as flat and empty as his eyes. Both, however, were far from lifeless.

She spent a brief moment being glad she'd have assistance when she finally released him. Suppressing a shiver as he continued to stare holes into her, she even admitted she'd miss his cocky, oh-so-cool sense of humor. It was better this way. *Yeah, but for who, Giardi?* "Fine," she said, the word sharper than intended. "Then we understand each other."

He said nothing. He didn't so much as nod. He simply stared at her.

She turned back toward the table, feeling his gaze every step of the way. It was time to unpack the rest of her gear and settle in for the duration. Eight days was not that long. She thought of the man lying naked, strapped to the bed less than ten yards away from her. The man whose body was a living sculpture of graceful power, the man whose dark eyes were a well of banked fury. No, eight days was not a long period of time, but at the moment, it seemed like an eternity.

Perhaps she had been a bit rash in threatening him. She knew her stuff. He couldn't get loose. She shouldn't have let his verbal tactics rattle her. But she had.

Keeping her back to the still silent, still staring, Blackstone, Scottie dragged her duffel over to the small kitchen counter and pulled out several boxes of power bars and several big tins of powdered protein drink. Next to that she tossed a bag of juice pouches. Her candy bars stayed in her pack. One never knew when a quick exit might be necessary. Where she went, they went.

She reached back in her bag just as the small gold stud in her right ear began to vibrate, signaling an incoming message from Del. She pulled out a small digital phone, then quickly slipped it in the waistband of her pants, tucked up under her shirt.

She debated feeding Blackstone before returning

Del's silent page. After their little tête-à-tête, mealtime could prove interesting. She almost looked forward to describing the menu. It all sat behind her on the counter. But it was barely sunrise. Blackstone could wait. That reminded her that they had yet to tackle the answering-nature's-call aspect of his incarceration.

Gee, the day looked to be filled with all sorts of fun and frolic. A dry smile crossed her face as she headed to the back door and let herself onto the deck. She could hardly wait.

She quickly dialed in the access code. After repeating a string of numbers, she waited for the return string. Once that was done, Del's voice came clearly into her ear. The joys of digital technology.

"You hummed. Sir." There was a short, censuring pause, but for once, she didn't feel chastised. She *was* team commander after all. No matter what Del's sudden reappearance indicated for her future, she knew she'd done a more than capable job of rebuilding his team. Her team. For the first time, she realized just how much she'd come to associate herself with her new role.

"Situation report?" came the terse request.

"Under control." She waited a moment, then asked, "Any further information on Logan Blackstone?"

There was a brief pause. "You have specific concerns?"

"He's had training above and beyond any local police department, even Detroit."

"Curiosity, Giardi?"

"Caution, sir." She knew he didn't buy that. Still, she had opened the subject. And she was curious enough to pursue it. "Your daughter had a contact with a former Detroit cop in New Mexico, didn't she? Vince Gerraro I think his name was. He'd have been on the force the same time as Blackstone. Might be worth a call."

"Unless you have a specific concern, I don't have the man power to put on that right now. You do have him contained, don't you?"

She clamped her jaw tight. "Yes, sir."

There was another brief pause. "I'll see what I can dig up." It wasn't a promise, but it was more than she'd hoped for. "You know better than anyone that we're stretched pretty thin."

"Apparently not as thin as I'd thought."

This time the pause wasn't one of consideration. There was no attempt to mask the hard edge to his tone. "There was no time to send the latest report through me. There is a messenger already en route to you, direct from the base site near the compound. It should be at station two in three hours. Can you rendezvous?"

Scottie glanced over her shoulder at the cabin, thinking of the man chained within. Station two was the location where she'd hidden the snowmobile. The round-trip would take her out of the cabin for approximately six hours. With less confidence than she should be feeling, she said, "I'll be there."

"I will update you again tomorrow by this link at twelve hundred hours. The link won't be operational at any other time. If you don't hear from me by then, clear out."

Scottie wondered how in the hell he expected her to clear out of a snowbound cabin with two hundred-plus pounds of recalcitrant hostage in tow, but didn't voice the question. If necessary, she'd find a way. And Del knew it.

That measure of trust should have eased some of the continued sting that Del's abrupt reentry had delivered. It did. But not enough to make it go away. She wasn't sure what that was going to take, but now was not the time to analyze it. Her emotions had been on more of a roller coaster in the past twenty-four hours than she'd allowed in many years. She wasn't ready to look too deeply at anything more at the moment.

"Yes, sir," she replied, then disconnected the call.

She tucked the phone back in her pants, then took advantage of the growing light to run a quick reconnaissance of the cabin. Satisfied that all was as usual, she went back inside.

Without wasting time, she immediately pulled on her parka. She grabbed three protein bars, stuffed two in her pocket and peeled the other as she walked determinedly into the bedroom.

"I will be gone for six hours. You might want to eat this." She held it close enough for him to take a bite. She'd purposely not focused directly on him, but the intensity of his gaze eventually pulled hers in.

"No bacon, huh?" The humor in his tone didn't reflect even a ripple of emotion in his flat eyes.

"Sorry. All out. Take it or wait until this afternoon."

"At which time I will have a different menu selection?"

She glared at him. "You have about thirty seconds. Decide."

He lifted his head the fraction of an inch necessary and took a bite. Scottie watched strong, white teeth clamp down on the chewy bar and tear off the end. She fought the urge to pull her fingertips farther away. When he clamped on the last inch or so, she let go, but was unable to tear her gaze away from the workings of his jaw. When he swallowed the last bite, she swallowed as well . . . in relief.

"I don't suppose I get water rations with this?"

Scottie wanted nothing better than to walk directly out of the cabin and straight down the mountain, but she couldn't. Without looking at him again, she walked to the kitchen and filled a small plastic tumbler with water. Keeping her thoughts on the hike ahead and the situation report that awaited her, she entered the bedroom and moved to the side of the bed.

He lifted his head slightly, and she tipped the cup carefully against his lips. His lips. Keeping her attention focused on his mouth made the action more intimate, not less. Her hand trembled, accidentally sending a trickle of water across his cheek and down his neck.

She pulled the glass away. "Sorry." She instinctively reached down to wipe the water off his skin. His cheek was rough with night-shadow, but it didn't diminish the heat searing her fingertips. She started to move her hand away, but he was faster, turning his head and capturing two of her fingers in his mouth. She tugged automatically, and he clamped gently down with his teeth. Her gaze flew to his. He held it without blinking. The subtle pressure of those perfect, white teeth on the gentle skin of her fingers should have been alarming. But the sensation skittering along the nerve endings in her hands and arms was anything but unpleasant.

Striving to maintain control, she kept her expression even. It cost her. "I'm sorry, but the meal portion of your breakfast is over."

He smiled without releasing her, then his eyes went all hot and smoky as he held her gaze and deliberately softened his hold so that his lips slid slowly off of her fingers, closing gently on her fingertips.

Scottie barely subdued the shudder of pleasure that begged to ripple throughout her body. She wasn't certain, but it was a pretty good bet that if she'd tried to take so much as a step at that moment, she would have exploded into a million tiny, electrified bits.

"More water?"

"Certainly." She tipped the cup over and poured the last ounce of water smack on his face.

He didn't react or even sputter. He just held her gaze.

Flustered and damning herself for letting him get to her, she turned and strode directly out of the cabin.

She was an hour and a half down the mountain when she remembered she hadn't given Blackstone a chance to answer nature's call. She smiled to herself, suddenly not feeling as guilty about pouring more water on him than in him.

Six hours turned into nine. The report, when the messenger finally made it to the site, hadn't been bad, but it hadn't been reassuring. No update from Lucas Blackstone in almost twenty-four hours. In a situation such as this, with an agent so deep under cover, it wasn't unusual to miss a contact point or two. But with the recent information of the Brethren's real plans, maintaining regular contact was more important than ever. Scottie could only hope that by the time Del contacted her at noon the next day, he would have further word.

It was late afternoon when Scottie arrived back at the cabin. Exhausted, hungry, and tired of drinking melted snow, she still took the time to run a circuit check of the area before heading inside. As she had when she'd first approached the cabin that morning—though it felt more like days ago now—she made enough tracks in the snow and in the surrounding woods to effectively cover the actual trail she'd made down the mountain.

As tired as she was, her senses still went on full alert the moment she stepped inside the cabin. She froze. Her neck prickled a warning alarm, but it was unnecessary. Someone was loose in the cabin.

There were no other tracks outside beside her own, she had made sure of that. The cabin was small enough so that she was certain no one else could have been hiding out. She knew there was no third person in this house. That could only mean one thing. She turned her head and looked into the bedroom.

The bed was empty.

THREE

Damn but it was colder than hell outside. Logan tucked the sheet a little tighter around his waist, wishing he'd had time to drag on a pair of jeans before sliding out the bedroom window. Wishes were for fools and dead men. He'd been the former, one more time than he cared to recall. He was convinced it was only because God had a perverse sense of humor that he had escaped becoming the latter.

He'd begun to appreciate that sense of humor two months before when his father had died in his arms, leaving behind an unexpected legacy. He had a brother. A twin brother.

On his dying breath Blackie had issued a challenge. Find Lucas. From any other man it would have been a final request. Blackie didn't make requests, nor did he issue orders. His methods were far more clever. Logan had been a grown man before he had understood them.

Blackie's motto had been, "Discover what motivates a person. Then use that desire to make them want to do what you wanted done all along." It was a very success-ful form of emotional blackmail. It worked even beyond the grave.

Logan moved slowly toward the back deck, keeping close to the side of the cabin. His feet hurt from the cold. He focused on that pain to keep his mind sharp. Whatever the hell she'd pumped into him that morning had left him fuzzy. The concentration he'd had to use to keep his confusion at bay had exhausted him.

Even so, he'd begun working on getting free the moment he'd heard her close the sliding door. Despite her obvious skill in utilizing restraints, he'd anticipated being free and tracking her before an hour had elapsed. But she was better than good. He owed his freedom more to luck than his own skill. He'd barely made it out the window as she'd opened the deck door.

After taking care of the pressure that had begun to feel like a jackknife in his bladder, he crept forward, angled his head very slightly, and peered around the edge of the sliding glass door with one eye. Snow blind-ness made it difficult to see anything but dark shadows. He didn't have the luxury of waiting for his pupils to adjust. Lord only knew what other nasty surprises she had in that damn black bag. He hated surprises.

A shadow moved into the bedroom. The light from the window highlighted his captor. Her hands were empty. She stepped immediately up onto the bed and went to the window. Smart. He had to be smarter. He tugged off the cumbersome sheet and made his move.

She waited a beat too long deciding whether to fol-low him out the window or backtrack to the glass door. She turned toward the door just as he came across the bed.

He pulled her backward, flipping her under him as they landed hard. She was facedown, her head turned to one side. He had her wrists pinned on her lower back, his knees on her spread thighs, and his mouth by her ear.

"I like a woman who's active in bed, but you really push things to the limit."

"Go to hell."

She didn't fight him, but he didn't for a second believe she'd accepted defeat. He kept his hold firm. "Been there, done that, didn't bother buying the T-shirt."

"Why, none big enough to fit over your ego?"

"Nah. I knew I'd get another chance on my next trip."

"I'll do my best to make that real soon."

"You can try." She craned her head just enough to hold his gaze. Hers was unwavering.

It was a helluva time to notice how incredibly green her eyes were. He was already well aware of the rest of her . . . attributes. Watching her athletic form as she strolled in and out of the bedroom, it had been impossible not to notice. Those black ski pants of hers fit like a second skin. Now she was pinned beneath him for the second time, all taut muscle and finely tuned response.

Yeah, she had him taut and finely tuned too. Adrenaline wasn't the only thing pumping through his system.

"How'd you get out of the restraints?" she asked, her voice steady and determined despite the strain of her current position.

"Professional curiosity?"

"Harry Houdini couldn't have gotten out of those straps."

"Martin Riggs could."

Her eyebrows quirked. "Never heard of him."

He let out a disgusted sigh. "What kind of cop are you, Detective?"

She didn't flinch, but he felt the tension in her wrists stretch even tighter.

"I'm not a cop." She briefly closed her eyes. They flashed open, the momentary blip in her otherwise complete control might have gone unnoticed had he not been watching her so intently. "Who's Martin Riggs?"

"You might not be a cop any longer, but you were. A detective, as I believe I deduced earlier."

She said nothing, her expression remained stony.

Oh, she was good. He was better. "As for Riggs, any self-respecting officer of the law watches cop shows. Martin Riggs was the Mel Gibson character in the *Lethal Weapon* movies."

She studied him for a second longer, then lifted her head a fraction and flicked a dismissive glance over his shoulders and chest before meeting his eyes once again. "Your ego really does need a reality check."

He almost smiled. "You're just mad because I'm on top this time." It occurred to him that he was actually enjoying himself. Big mistake.

"Don't get used to it," she shot back.

His lips quirked. "Hey, I'm a sensitive guy. I let the woman be in control. Occasionally."

"Let?"

"Now whose ego is bruised? What's the matter, Detective Princess, you don't like giving up control?" He pressed his lips a little closer to her ear. "No matter what women say, they like being pulled beneath a nice, hard body, they like feeling the weight of their man settle between their legs." He relaxed his weight more heavily on her thighs. "But not you, right?"

Had he really heard that soft intake of breath? When he'd made the tactical error of pressing too much of him against too much of her, it became hard to hear past the thrumming in his own ears.

For all her trim muscle and smart mouth, her body felt pliant beneath him. He redoubled his concentration and worked on steadying his heart rate. She'd tricked him once before. He might be enjoying this unexpected, if intriguing twist in his hunt for Lucas, but he wouldn't let it interfere with his ultimate goal. He sighed. Playtime was over.

He didn't pull away, deciding the position lent more advantage than disadvantage. For the moment, anyway.

"Why don't we dispense with all the bondage foreplay and get to the main act," he said. The amusement disappeared, his tone was cool and sharp. "What do you want with me?"

Scottie swore silently. She should have kept him talking, kept him preoccupied and focused on his sudden reversal of power until she found the weak link. She doubted he'd let her take him as easily as before, and her current position didn't lend itself to many possibilities.

Then he'd dropped his already deep voice to that rough whisper and painted visions in her mind that were all too clear and none too safe. Damn her. Even exhausted as she was, she'd responded—with great enthusiasm.

She could have made excuses for herself by pointing out that any woman with two-hundred pounds of beautifully sculpted, aroused, naked male above her would have to have been dead not to react, but she didn't. Scottie didn't make excuses. Not for herself, not for her team.

So why was there this tiny, niggling sense of relief picking its way into her brain? Relief? Just because she'd responded like a healthy, sexual human being?

Exactly.

"You didn't answer my question," she said, as much to keep him talking as to distract herself from that train of thought. "How did you get out of the restraints? Or should I ask," she added mockingly, "how did Mel do it?"

"Riggs could dislocate his shoulder."

"On purpose? You can do that?"

"No. But I am double-jointed."

"Handy."

She felt his breath caress her, tickling her ear. "It has its moments."

That quivering sensation rushed over her skin again. "I bet." Scottie wasn't so sure having proof that her sexuality still existed was such a relief after all. Being in thrall to her hormones was a unique experience that would make for interesting analysis, but not right now.

Yet she seemed to have no choice. Every breath he expelled, every tiny movement he made caused a reaction in her. She was excruciatingly aware of every contact point between them, even the feel of the mattress beneath her.

His fingers tightened slightly around her wrists. She was a tall woman with a frame to match, yet his hand easily encompassed both of her wrists with a strength that did not need to be exerted to be understood. She heard his whisper again in her mind. *They like feeling the weight of their man between their legs.* Indeed the weight of his body on hers wasn't at all unpleasant. It made concentrating on anything but the sensations he was causing inside her all but impossible.

Stop! she commanded herself. *Think.* She couldn't very well lie beneath him on a bed and keep him talking for eight days. *And nights*, her mind inserted helpfully.

She stifled a groan. Battling him was a difficult enough challenge. She did not need to battle herself as well.

"Enough about me," he said. "Let's talk about you."

"Let me up," she instructed. "We can talk in the kitchen after you've dressed."

"You give orders very well. Does that come from being the detective? Or the princess?"

"I've never been a princess of any kind in my life."

"Oh, you went straight to queen then. How plebeian of me. Please forgive me Your Highness."

Scottie didn't know whether to laugh or scream in frustration. Even in his condescension there was no cruelty. In fact, there was an underlying amusement in most everything he said that begged her to join him in his mockery. Considering she was the target, it should have been easier to resist. She had to work at it.

"Fancy speech for a cop. Or does that come from playing bartender-philosopher?"

His smile remained, but the light went out in his eyes. She could have shivered from the chill. It was much easier now to recall the dark specter that had loomed over her an hour before. Sarah. Scottie wondered again who she was, this woman who had the ability to make him lose control.

Without warning, Logan flipped her on her back.

She was not a small woman. His power and the ease with which he exerted it made her realize again just how lucky she'd been earlier.

He straddled her, his ankles pressing hers to the bed to keep her legs straight so she couldn't rear up. Her wrists were still pinned at the base of her spine by his hand, the uncomfortable position made worse as it cocked her hips at an awkward—not to mention disturbingly intimate—angle.

His other hand captured a fistful of hair. He leaned down. His black eyes glittered, giving his smile an almost evil cast. The dark specter had returned.

"Who the hell are you? How do you know me?"

This menacing side of him made her relax. Bullies and madmen she could handle. She had a lifetime of experience with their kind.

"Let me up and I'll tell you," she said calmly.

He reared back and tugged her half off the bed. With her hands and arms immobile, she had no balance and was forced to brace her chest against his. Their faces were less than an inch apart.

His smile disappeared. When he spoke, his voice was a growling whisper. "Now." He nodded to the straps tangled on the sheets. "Unless you want to see if you're double-jointed too."

"Try it."

His eyes widened, then the smile returned. She'd surprised him. Good. She had no chance in her current situation. She doubted mentioning Sarah would throw him again. She had to get him to move off of her.

"You like living dangerously," he said.

"I'm here, aren't I?"

He said nothing. Then, very deliberately, he

dropped his gaze to her mouth. After a long moment when she could almost taste her pulse in her throat, he looked up at her through thick black eyelashes.

"Why, yes. Yes, you are."

His voice, those eyes, the weight of his body . . . his naked body. He was the perfect male animal; finely tuned, supremely controlled, and quite comfortable in nothing more than his own skin. He was seduction personified, and she was damned sure he knew it.

He smiled slowly as if reading her mind. A small gasp slipped past her lips. She quelled the sudden panic knotting her stomach. Bring back the bully, she schooled herself, bring back the madman.

"Trust me," she said, fighting to keep her voice calm, unaffected. "If I'd come up here looking for something"—she glanced down, then back up—"personal, I wouldn't have needed the syringe. I don't drug my men."

She'd played the role of femme fatale before in order to fight off unwanted attention. It had always been easy. Of course the key word in those cases was "unwanted." This was different. This was like playing around a fire with an unlit firecracker. And she was the firecracker.

"I'd say whatever drove you to climb a mountain after a blizzard in order to attack a naked man in his bed, needle or no needle, sounds pretty damn personal. I sure took it personally." He slowly lowered her back down to the bed, following her until she was pinned beneath the full length of his body. Her hands were still caught behind her. He was heavy . . . and hard. His hips pressed deeply into hers.

There was no controlling her reaction. It was instinctive, primal. She pushed back. A groan caught in her throat.

"Tell me what you want, princess," he said, his voice hot and silky. "Or would you like me to show you what you want?"

What she wanted was him off of her. *Dear God, she wanted him inside of her.*

He pressed down again, making her swallow a gasp. He smiled. "The hell with it. I'll show you what I want. We can talk later." He lowered his mouth.

She wanted to taste his lips so badly, she literally ached. But this was business, dammit. She was on the job.

He'd somehow narrowed the entire world down to the breath of space between his lips and hers. She couldn't concentrate, couldn't think of anything else but him and what he was doing to her, what he was making her feel. *Heaven have mercy*, she wanted to beg him. Only she didn't know quite what she'd be begging for. "Don't."

He stilled, then pulled back a fraction, studying her.

She wanted to sigh in relief. She wanted to sob in aching frustration.

In that instant he rolled off of her to stand by the bed. Stunned by her sudden release, it took her a moment to switch gears. Her hand went immediately to her hip.

"Looking for this?"

He was by the door now. She stared without meaning to, certainly without wanting to, unable to contain the pulse of admiration that shot through her. Lounging in the doorway, naked and apparently unconcerned about that fact, he was an incredible male animal. An armed male animal. Her gun dangled carelessly from his thumb and forefinger.

She automatically reached for her ankle.

"Got that one too." He lifted his other hand, which held her knife.

She'd never felt a thing. Actually, she'd been feeling many things, too many things, unfortunately, and none of them were job related. Dammit, where was her head? He could have killed her. Several times.

Her only remaining weapon was sarcasm. "Let me guess, Mel Gibson's character was a pickpocket too?"

"I prefer sleight-of-hand artist. Don Johnson."

"The guy from *Miami Vice?*"

He sighed. "*Nash Bridges.* When was the last time you watched TV, anyway?"

"I stopped watching TV when *Hawaii Five-O* was canceled."

"Ah, a classics snob. You don't know what you've missed."

"You can't top perfection," she said. "*Mission Impossible, The Mod Squad, The Avengers.*"

"Yeah, but you also had stuff like *Dragnet.*"

She frowned. "Don't knock *Dragnet.*"

"*Get Smart,*" he challenged.

"Excellent satirical commentary," she responded with a sniff.

"Oh, please. Next you'll be telling me that *Charlie's Angels* was a platform for the women's movement."

"And you'll be telling me you watch *Baywatch* for the lifesaving techniques. You can't name three shows in the last ten years that could touch *Columbo.*"

"*Hill Street Blues. Barney Miller. Cagney and Lacey.*"

She paused, found herself actually suppressing a smile into a frown. "Okay, I'll give you those."

"Not to mention *NYPD Blue* or *Homicide*."

From the corner of her eye she spied the syringe. It was on the floor near the corner that angled to her right, hidden from his view by the bed. If she could keep him talking . . . "Wouldn't know. Don't watch them. Bring back *The Rockford Files* or *Baretta*, then maybe I'll tune in."

He shook his head, then shifted his weight, settling in for the debate. It was as big an opening as she was likely to get. Without tipping her hand by so much as a blink, she tucked and rolled backward off the bed, landing in a crouch.

Her best hope was to engage him in hand-to-hand combat. Going for the needle was just an excuse to make him move away from the door. It worked.

He was quick, launching himself in a flying tackle across the bed as she lunged for the syringe. It wouldn't stop a bullet, but she really didn't think he would shoot her. Not yet, anyway.

He caught her ankle and pulled her away just as her hand slapped down close to the syringe.

"Missed it by that much," he said in a perfect imitation of Don Adams's Agent 86.

She choked on a surprised laugh, giving up what edge she might have had. A second later she was pinned beneath him once again.

"You know, I'm beginning to think you really like this."

She was breathless, as much from frustration as exhaustion. She worked up a casual smile. "Tell you what, why don't we put all the toys away. You grab some sweats, and we'll go out to the table, have some dinner and talk. All this wrestling has made me hungry."

"You're offending my masculinity. I thought you were enjoying my natural self."

"Arnold Schwarzenegger couldn't offend your masculinity," she said, struggling against his superior weight even though she knew it wouldn't do any good. "Come on, you win. Two pins out of three. Now be a good sport and let me up."

He grinned down at her. "Wanna go for best three out of five."

She glared at him. "No. I'm crying uncle here, okay? You win. You're king of the sandbox. You get to keep all the toys." She bucked at him again. "Now get off of me."

"Squirming like that isn't helping your case any," he said, his voice husky. "I know an even better way to work up an appetite." He leaned closer. "It's sort of like wrestling, but you'll have to take your clothes off too."

She struggled not to swallow visibly as erotic images of the two of them entwined, naked, writhing on the floor assaulted her mind. How did he do that to her? She'd been propositioned more times than she could count and never, not once, had it affected her this way. So instantly. So . . . graphically.

"Even sex for sex's sake requires trust." She forced a slow smile, certain he could feel the trembling of her inner thighs. "You sure you can trust me even that much?"

He leaned closer. "Let's just say I'm willing to accept the challenge."

She held his gaze. "Throw the gun and the knife up on the bed."

His eyebrows lifted. She'd surprised him again. Hell, she'd surprised herself. *Just what are you going to do if this doesn't work?*

He pinned her hands with one of his, then picked up the gun he'd dropped when he tackled her and tossed both it and the knife on the bed. "Okay." He looked up. "Wait a minute." He leaned over her, his bare chest sliding across her face as he reached above her head. The syringe hit the bed a second later. He settled back down on top of her, straddling her hips, pinning her legs with his ankles. He slid her hands down until each wrist was beside her head. "No more needles. What next?"

She didn't move. When he'd loomed over her, she'd made the mistake of looking down. He was definitely, um, up for the job. She felt him . . . resting on her stomach. She kept her gaze locked on his.

At least she'd accomplished one thing. They were both unarmed. She'd leveled the playing field.

He smiled. Her pulse doubled. Muscles that she had no control over clutched painfully between her thighs.

Well, maybe it was still slanted a little, she reluctantly admitted. "I guess the first challenge will be getting my clothes off," she said.

"Looks like I tossed away the knife too soon."

A thrill shot through her at the thought of him slicing clothes from her body. He made her feel . . . wicked.

No, her little voice corrected. *He makes you feel alive.*

Maybe it was *she* who needed a challenge. As if single-handedly rebuilding her entire team hadn't been challenge enough. That, however, had been professional.

She stared into his black eyes and knew the truth of it. This—he—was personal.

For the past ten years, personal and professional had meant the same thing to her. The team. Work. Since joining them she'd worked solo and was content with that arrangement. Every need she allowed herself to have, the team fulfilled.

She continued to stare into his eyes and felt starved. In fact, she couldn't stop the thought that she'd never been so hungry in all her life.

"Then again," he said, his voice no more than a purr, "keep looking at me that way and clothing or the lack thereof can become optional."

She'd started this as a strategy to gain her freedom. Now all she could think about was what his hands would feel like on her. What would he feel like inside of her?

She swallowed in a desperate attempt to wet her throat.

He lowered his head. She felt his breath on her lips. He was going to kiss her. *Stop this before it's too late.* Why was he taking so long? His eyes were half-closed, his lips warm when they brushed hers. Her eyes began to drift shut.

He lifted his head a fraction. "Wait a minute."

Startled, she opened her eyes. *Some strategy, Giardi.* "Stalling, Blackstone?"

"You don't bite, do you?"

"Only when provoked."

He chuckled. It made her shiver. Damn him.

"Cold?" he asked, though he had to know she was anything but. "You're the one with all the clothes on."

"I thought you were going to remedy that."

"Must have lost my head."

"It's time I started to use mine." Without warning, she rammed her forehead up under his chin. Fortunately it worked, his head jerked backward and he released her hands. She didn't stop to ponder what would have happened to her if he hadn't let go.

Following through on the motion, she hooked her ankle around his and flipped him over, then clawed her way onto the bed. He recovered quickly and rolled to a crouch, ready to pounce.

She leveled the gun and fired. The bullet hit the wall beside his head. He froze. She lowered her aim to directly between his legs.

"Get dressed."

FOUR

"Most women just say no." Logan rubbed his jaw and worked hard to keep her in focus as lights winked in his peripheral vision. She'd administered a chin jab you didn't learn from a training manual, but he'd be damned before he let her know how effective it had been. Hell, if he was honest, he'd admit she'd already had his head spinning before she had tried to coldcock him.

"I thought you'd figured out I'm not most women. Be thankful I didn't go for your nose. That was my first choice." She slid backward off the bed, then moved around to the end. Ten feet separated them. "Get dressed."

Her demeanor was as no-nonsense as her tone, the gun was as steady as her gaze. If he hadn't been half of the intimate twosome they'd just made on the floor, he'd have never believed she was capable of gasping in pleasure-seeking anticipation. "My clothes are under the bed."

"Slide the bag out with your foot where I can see it."

He did so, careful to move slowly. "You know, I don't think I've ever been forced to put my clothes *on* at gunpoint."

"First time for everything."

He toed open the zipper flap, keeping his eyes on hers. She didn't so much as glance at the duffel bag. He didn't regret his professionally unwise tussle, and doubted he'd do things differently if given another chance. Well, he might kiss her first next time. If he lived that long.

"Move the bag back toward the wall next to you and slowly pull out the bare essentials. Try anything funny, and I'll shoot the first body part I can aim this gun at."

He didn't believe her. She wasn't going to shoot him. She didn't seem to want to hurt him. A broken nose was the least of the damage she could have inflicted on him, but she hadn't even done that.

No, she apparently wanted him whole and healthy. For what, he had no idea. He didn't need to be the one on top to get his answers.

"And let me guess," he said as he shoved the bag toward the wall with his foot, "you were first in your class at the firing range."

"I was the range instructor."

He slowly bent down, keeping his eyes on hers, and felt around for his jeans. "What force were you with?"

"One item at a time, and I want to see it."

He didn't expect an answer, but it was worth a try. He pulled a pair of worn blue jeans out and straightened.

"Toss them to me."

"I took all the string and frogs out of my pockets already, Ma." They landed on the bed beside her. She scooped them up one-handed and draped them over her shoulder, feeling the pockets and seams before tossing them back to him, never once breaking eye contact.

He caught them. "Do you want to feel up my under-wear too?"

"Just get dressed."

Fairly confident she wouldn't put a bullet in him—yet—he broke eye contact and bent to his bag. He felt her watching him as he pulled out briefs and a thickly woven, deep green rugby shirt.

"Give me the shirt. Put on your underwear and pants. No socks."

"Barbarian. My feet are still cold." He tossed the shirt to her, and she patted it down as he pulled on his other clothes. He caught her return toss and pulled the shirt on, leaving it untucked, the long tails hanging down to his thighs.

"Going barefoot in the snow was your own brilliant idea."

He smacked his forehead. "Gee, what was I thinking? I could have stayed in my nice, warm bed, strapped in all nice and cozy. Silly me."

"We can return to that arrangement, but that means another needle."

He barely covered a flinch. "Thanks, but no."

She waved her gun at him. "Walk, hands at your sides."

She stayed a good ten feet behind him. Very well trained, he thought. With her reflexes, even a rear flying kick from that distance would probably miss her. A bullet from the same distance would not miss him.

"Stand beside the couch. There," she said, pointing with her free hand.

"You missed your calling, you know," he said, following directions as casually as he thought he could get away with. His nonchalant attitude irked her, even if she didn't show it. It was a small weapon, but over time it could be very effective. He wondered how much time he had.

"Put these on." She pulled a pair of standard issue handcuffs from her bag and tossed them to him. "And what calling was that?"

He hadn't expected her to follow up. "Curiosity, Detective Princess?"

"Analysis, Lieutenant."

"I'm not a lieutenant. I'm a bartender, remember?"

"You're a lot of things, Blackstone. Right now what you are is under my protection. Put on the cuffs."

He put the cuffs on, eyeing her with a taunting smile as he pushed them to a fairly tight slot.

Her only reaction was to toss him a pair of ankle cuffs with a long chain between them. "These too, Houdini. Chain over the handcuffs."

"Boy, you really have a thing for bondage, don't you?" He sat on the couch. He snapped one cuff on, looped the chain over the links between his wrists, then put on the other cuff. He made sure his jeans were tucked into the cuffs. No use in carving up more skin than he had to. "I can't wait to find out what else you have in your toy bag there. Whips?"

The hint of a real smile was buried beneath her dry response. "Sorry, I left them at home this trip."

"Lucky me." He shifted his back to the armrest and swung his legs up onto the couch, making as much noise as possible. He took his time settling in, then said, "So, you say I'm under your protection. I gotta tell you, you have a really unique way of protecting people, Detective." The frown lines carved deeper into her forehead every time he called her that. He planned to call her that often.

"Not everyone realizes they require protecting." She pulled out a chair and sat facing him.

Less than ten feet separated them now, but the gun resting on her knee kept him pinned to the couch. "Well, I guess I definitely fall into that category. Who are you protecting me from, Detective? And who's going to protect me from you?"

She stood. "I'm starving."

"You've drugged me, beaten me, and chained me up. Don't you think I at least deserve to know why I was so lucky to qualify for your generous protection services?"

Turning her back to him, she walked to the small counter in the kitchen where she'd stored her supplies. She kept the gun. There was no way he could move more than an inch without the chains alerting her to the fact. It was basic captive restraint, but simple was often the most effective.

"I like my steak medium rare," he said.

"I don't cook." She pulled a foil-wrapped power bar out of the box on the counter and tossed it at him. It landed on his outstretched thighs, right in front of his fingers.

"Good aim, Detective."

She smiled. "A wise thing to remember." A juice pouch followed, landing in exactly the same spot.

Logan shook his head and tore open the foil wrapper. In the past two months his entire being had been exclusively focused on one thing: finding his brother. In hunting him down, he'd discovered that Lucas didn't want to be found, but he did need to be rescued. His twin had been brainwashed by some lunatic fringe cult, operating up in the mountains somewhere. He couldn't fathom how anyone could let themselves get so messed up that they could be swayed by these fanatics, but that didn't matter right now. He'd save Lucas, whether his brother wanted to be saved or not.

He was all Logan had left. He wouldn't lose Lucas. He couldn't.

So why was he sitting there, chained up, eating cardboard food and actually enjoying himself? He chewed slowly and watched his captor, who was rooting in her black bag of tricks. He should be going ape, being trapped the way he was. Instead he found he was more than content to watch the good detective. He'd never met a woman like her. He was both captive and captivated.

He shook his head and popped the last bite into his mouth. Maybe he'd finally lost it. Maybe when you lost your mind it didn't make you crazy with pain, as he'd long suspected—expected. Maybe it just made you crazy. Suddenly it wasn't so hard to fathom the weak-minded after all.

He raised his eyebrows as she sat back in the chair and unwrapped another candy bar. The look of bliss that briefly crossed her face as she chewed the first bite stirred a hunger of a completely different kind in him. He shifted slightly on the couch. The sound of his chains made her eyes snap back open.

"So, how come you get chocolate and I get fused pasteboard?"

"It's good for you. Chocolate will rot your teeth."

"You've got an answer for everything, Detective, except the questions I most want answers to."

"Sorry. And stop calling me detective." She turned her back to him, pulled another small stash from her bag, and carried it to the counter.

"You don't like Detective Princess? I'm wounded. And here I thought I was being charming and sociable, not to mention creative and incredibly observant. All of which I deserve credit for, seeing as you're being so rude to me. Don't you think so, Detective? It is detective, isn't it?"

She slammed a box on the counter then looked upward, her eyes closed. "Scottie," she said with exaggerated calm.

"I don't think he can beam you up from here, Captain. No' enough power."

She groaned. He smiled. He thought his burr was pretty good. Considering his Scots father was only a second-generation American, it should be. A sharp pang pinched his heart at the thought of Blackie. Now the only third-generation American Blackstone was Logan. And Lucas.

Scottie turned and leaned against the counter, her hands braced on either side of her. The gun was still at her fingertips. "*My* name is Scottie. Are you happy?"

He pushed aside the resident ache in his heart and focused on his current plan of attack. "Happy? No. I'm Logan. Though I think the dwarves had a pretty good thing going there. Seven guys, one woman. Hey, you wanna play Snow White?" He lifted his hands, rattling his chains. "I'll be Sleazy."

She curled her fingers into fists and turned slowly back to unpacking.

He grinned. Goading her was a strategic plan, but he had to admit he was enjoying the role. She was fun to rile up. He supposed it was because she was a worthier adversary than he'd come up against in . . . well, in too many years to count. Sarah's smile taunted the fringes of his mind. He shoved those memories away too.

His smile was slightly more forced when he said, "I'm getting to you, aren't I? Women say I drive them crazy."

"This is not a surprise." She faced him again. "Though I wouldn't sound so smug. There's a difference between lust-crazed and just plain crazed."

In response, Logan took a leisurely visual inventory, his gaze finally settling back on her face. Her flat expression faltered. "You speaking from personal experience?"

She crossed her arms. "Only on the latter."

He dropped his voice to a dark whisper. "Liar."

She stiffened, but to her credit her skin didn't flush. He was mildly disappointed by that. He realized he wanted her more than just bothered. He wanted her hot and bothered.

"I'd say you have more pressing things to worry about than whether you can seduce me." She shot a pointed look at his ankle and wrist chains. "Regardless of what you might have been led to believe, bondage does nothing for me."

"On the contrary," he said, "seeing as I am chained and you won't talk to me about the details of my incarceration, I have little left to do other than indulge in my fantasies."

She crossed the short space to the table and hefted

her black pack. *"Penthouse* will no doubt be thrilled with your next letter."

He watched her as she moved to the small refrigerator and lifted the pack on top of it. Chained as he was, even if he was allowed mobility in the cabin, he'd be lucky to reach the handle of the fridge, much less anything higher. The only thing she'd left within easy reach were power bars. Boxes of them. Oh yum.

"Just how long do you plan on keeping me here?" He shifted his back and carefully crossed one leg over the other.

The sound of the heavy links clanking made her pause. After a moment, she said, "Eight to ten days. And don't even think about moving." She went into the bedroom.

His eyes widened, more because he'd finally gotten some information out of her than at the answer itself. "A man can't live on power bars alone," he called to her.

She was a real mystery, one he'd love to spend time solving. Unfortunately, he didn't have a week to spend deciphering her clues. He figured he had another two days before he could hike farther up and continue his search for the best entry into the compound where Lucas was being held. Two days was plenty of time to get himself out of this mess and find out what the hell she was doing. It didn't take a rocket scientist to figure out it had something to do with his search for Lucas.

What in the hell have you gotten yourself into, Brother, if the government has agents out after you?

"Lucky for you, you have all those fantasies to keep you occupied," she responded.

Smiling again, he leaned forward so he could see

her. She was retrieving his hiking boots from under the bed. The semiautomatic was on the bed within easy reach.

He waited until she'd finished checking out the room. She was quite thorough. She grabbed his bag and boots and carried them to the kitchen table.

He shifted, rattling his chains a little. She looked up. When her eyes met his, he said, "Thinking about those fantasies will only make me hungrier."

He watched her hold herself even more still, keeping her gaze emotionless, but the swallow she took belied her disaffected pretense.

"I make you crave more than chocolate, don't I, Scottie?"

He wished he was closer, wished he could see her green eyes, watch her pupils dilate in reaction. It was the only one she couldn't control. His gaze drifted down, snagging on her tight black turtleneck. His body twitched. There was one other reaction she couldn't control either. He looked back into her eyes. "I won't rot your teeth either, princess."

He noticed her white-knuckled grip on the table. He lifted his wrists. "Why don't you take these things off of me?" He nodded to the window. "I can't go anywhere anyway." He had several dozen questions he wanted to demand answers to, not the least of which was how in the hell had she gotten to the cabin after a blizzard. But right at that moment, none of those questions seemed to matter. He wanted to get his hands on her . . . but not to force her to talk.

No, he didn't want to *force* her to do anything.

"You want me to stay here, fine. You say you are only protecting me. You must be telling the truth, or you would have done more damage to me by now. You've had ample opportunity. Hell, you had me dead walking in the bedroom door."

He didn't have to be close to see her reaction to that reminder. Only he didn't think her slight intake of breath was due to her thinking about him dying. Just how long had she been standing there, staring at him, naked in his bed?

"I'd like some answers, but I won't hurt you in order to get them." He held his wrists out. "Cut me loose, Scottie."

Scottie stared at him. "You really are crazy."

"We're both professionals." At her raised brow, he added, "We've both been cops at one point in our lives. We know this drill, both of us."

"Which is precisely why you should know better than to ask me to let you go."

"Scottie, I—"

She cut him off by turning her back to him and began searching his duffel bag. "There's more than one way to hurt a person," she said quietly.

Logan started to shoot off a reply, then stopped himself. Something about those softly spoken words caught at him. He thought back over their conversation. He'd promised no physical violence. He'd also propositioned her with personal pleasure.

The quick conclusion he made bothered him. He also had a strong suspicion his instincts were on target. In his hunt for Lucas he'd discovered he hadn't lost any of what had made him a good detective. Good detective. He stifled a self-deprecating snort, squashed the sharp dagger of guilt that accompanied it.

Good detectives didn't get their witnesses killed. They didn't fall in love with them either.

He stared hard at Scottie. She fascinated the hell out of him. And yes, he desired to know her more intimately. It had been a very, very long time since he'd felt both for the same person. In fact, not since Sarah had he—

He shut down. What in the hell was he doing? Wasn't it bad enough that he'd somehow drawn the attention of another private government agency? Obviously Lucas was into something a lot deeper than selling daisies at airports. Even with the information he had access to, Logan had come up hard against an impenetrable wall when trying to dig into the Brethren. He knew next to nothing about them. He'd tracked Lucas to their door, so to speak, then poof! Nothing.

Scottie had information he needed, he'd bank on it. She was no lackey sent to guard the intruder. Instead of playing games and looking at her as a hormonal diversion while he waited for the snow to melt, he should be doing whatever was necessary to make her talk. If that meant hurting her or seducing her, so be it. After all, she hadn't exactly been too concerned about his rights, civil or otherwise.

He continued to watch her. He didn't want to hurt her. He did want to seduce her. Sarah's face loomed before him again. Only this time she wasn't smiling. Her face was frozen in an eternal mask of surprised pain, her eyes open but unseeing.

Logan closed his eyes. *Damn.* Too many ghosts in his life.

He opened his eyes. Scottie was systematically going through every inch of his bag, stacking up clothes on one side, hardware on the other. No, he didn't want to hurt her. Which was precisely why he wouldn't seduce her.

He would get the information out of her, though. One way or the other. To that end, his strategy of annoying her into talking to him had actually been fairly effective.

But even that path was denied him when she said, "It's been a long day. You have ten minutes in the bathroom, then you can take the bed."

"It's barely seven o'clock."

"Ten minutes," she replied. She turned her attention to stowing his clothes back in his bag. She kept the hardware.

He started to balk, but recalling the urgency of how he'd spent his morning hours, Logan moved off the couch to the bathroom. When he emerged exactly ten minutes later, she was standing beside the couch.

He opened his mouth, intending to say something, anything, to goad her, but there was an almost hollow look around her eyes, a weary pull at the corners of her mouth. Now was the time to pummel away at her, wear her down, force her to make a mistake. Then he could make his move, though no matter the extent of her exhaustion, he knew it would never be an easy battle. There were a thousand questions to be answered.

Yet he found himself asking none of them. "I'll take the couch," he said.

She eyed him warily. Apparently fatigue hadn't dulled her instincts. "I appreciate the gallant gesture," she said dryly, "but the bed is yours." She raised a hand to forestall his response. "I realize the couch might be more comfortable in your present condition, but I can guard you more effectively if you take the bed."

Logan spent several long seconds debating his own instincts, eventually quashing them before moving to the bedroom doorway. He would get his answers. First thing tomorrow morning.

He paused before going inside, several pointed comments rising to the tip of his tongue. At the last minute, he swallowed them and simply said, "Good night."

As he settled himself on the bed, feeling her gaze on him every second, he told himself he'd called a truce because he knew it would drive her crazy, making her unable to rest for wondering why he'd given in so easily. He was surprised at the sleepiness that immediately tugged at him the moment his head nestled into the pillow. An image of Scottie, lines of fatigue etching her face, a slight slump to her broad shoulders, her spine overly stiff to compensate for it, swam before his closed eyes. And he knew why he'd really called a truce.

As sleep seduced him under her spell, he released a long sigh. She was watching over him. And for this once, he knew his dreams would be pleasant ones.

When he woke up, the sun was well over the horizon. He couldn't remember the last time he'd slept so deeply, much less for so long. In that waking realization, he had immediate and full cognizance of where he was and why . . . and what condition he was in. It was then he noticed the heavy blanket lying smoothly over him. Chained and shackled, yet he'd slept like the dead. He raised his gaze and spotted Scottie standing beside the couch. She was up and dressed, either in the same clothes she had had on yesterday or ones just like them. Black was definitely her color.

He felt an immediate tug. That it was more an emotional one than a purely physical one, had him climbing awkwardly from the bed without asking permission. Truce time was over.

"You're up," she said, as he came into the main room.

Hearing her smoky voice had an odd, unexpected effect on him. She sounded warm, cozy . . . inviting. It was a voice he decided he could easily wake up to every morning. He looked at her, then simply nodded and headed, chains rattling, to the bathroom. He needed a few more minutes to wake up.

She was at the kitchen counter when he came out. A quick glance around told him where she'd slept. The couch had been shifted slightly to give her visual access to the bedroom.

He pictured her, curled up on the couch, watching him as he slept. It didn't bother him the way it should have. No, the thought of her falling asleep while watching him didn't seem to bother him at all.

Then he noticed a blanket balled up in one corner and a pillow that looked as if it had been used for punching practice. Apparently she hadn't fallen asleep watching him. But a long, sleepless night for her was a good thing for him. Funny, but he had a hard time reconciling himself to that fact.

It was a bit easier when he realized what she was doing. She was cleaning a gun. His gun.

"Scottie?"

"What?" she said, sparing him a brief glance.

"What is that short for anyway?"

She snapped the magazine into his Glock and chambered a bullet. She aimed across the room and sighted down the barrel. "Anunsciata."

She'd surprised him again by answering. And what an answer. He whistled. "Hell of a moniker, princess."

She scowled at him. "Scottie. You asked. Use it."

Oh, I plan to, he said silently. *I plan to.* "Your family Catholic, huh?"

"My mother was."

"Your father must have loved her to let her hang that on you. I'm almost afraid to ask what your last name is."

"The only thing my father loved was the force. It was his life, his mistress, his wife, and his religion." She laid the gun down and faced him. Her expression was as blank and empty as her tone had been. "You got a permit for this thing?"

"Uncle Sam is sending out field agents to track down unregistered handguns now?" She didn't so much as blink. He sighed, wishing she weren't such a compelling puzzle. She kept giving him pieces but none of them seemed to fit together. He hated puzzles. Until he solved them. She folded her arms, waiting. "Yes," he said finally, "I have a permit. It's in my wallet."

"Which is where?"

He shrugged. "I don't feel a real warm sense of sharing here."

She shrugged. "It's a cruel world, Blackstone."

"Not even a simple trade?"

"I doubt there is anything in your wallet that will give me information I don't already have, so your bargaining power is slim to none."

"Can you tell me why the government is suddenly so

interested in a guy hanging out in an old cabin in Montana?"

"Who says I work for the government? I thought I was a cop?"

He lifted his hands, palms up. The chains clanked together. "Listen, why don't we cut the bull, okay?"

She smiled. "I don't recall being the one shoveling it."

"You know a lot about me. You're not local. I think I have you pegged pretty well. And I also think we both know what the common bond is here, so I'll stop the wordplay and treat you like the highly trained pro you are, if you'll give me the same courtesy."

"A highly trained pro doesn't relay information without good reason. You haven't given me one of those."

"Yet."

She folded her arms. "What is this common bond? Put that on the table."

Logan didn't answer right away. He knew damn well she was there because of Lucas. But until he knew more about why they wanted to keep him "protected," he wasn't about to offer his brother's name up on a platter.

She shifted away from the table. "I guess we're at a standstill then."

Logan took a different tack. "Why a week? What happens in a week?"

"I walk out of here, and we never see each other again."

"Did it occur to you that as a U.S. citizen I have rights that are being seriously abused?"

"So sue me."

"I just might do that."

"I should tell you, I'm not in the phone book. But if you can track me down and tell me what courtroom to be in, I'll be there."

Impatience reared its fiery head, with frustration fanning the flames. It brought back all the low points of his former career in a vivid recollection. He hadn't dealt well with those emotions then. He'd done slightly better since Sarah's death.

Yeah, quitting the force before he was thrown off was a hell of a way to manage stress.

Well, he wasn't on the force now. He didn't have to play by the rules.

Logan pulled his shackled feet under him and rose. She had the gun cocked and aimed before he'd fully straightened.

"Take these off of me." He once again held out his wrists.

"I thought we weren't playing games anymore."

"Exactly." He walked toward her.

She raised the aim from his chest to his forehead. "Stop right where you are."

He continued to walk toward her. "I'm done. Either take these damn chains off or shoot me."

"A stupid thing to die over, Blackstone. Stop now and you won't be harmed."

There was less than five feet between them. She had braced her legs and held the gun in a two-handed grip. The table was at the back of her thighs. One more step, and she'd have no choice but to give it up or shoot him.

He took another step.

She fired the gun.

FIVE

The bullet whizzed just over the top of Logan's head and embedded itself in the cabin wall with a loud pop.

"Are you sure you were the range instructor?"

Scottie blinked at him, the gun still held in front of her. *The idiot had actually made her shoot at him twice now!* That stunned moment of thought cost her.

Without warning, Logan swung his chained fists up and knocked her hands to the side. The gun went flying across the room, landing with a clatter by the bedroom door. Scottie lunged sideways onto the table, trying to avoid his attack and reach for the other gun. Logan came right after her. The table splintered under the force of their joined weight, and they went down in a heap. The broken pieces stabbed at her back and shoulders. Logan landed on his side in a sprawl atop her torso and legs, knocking the wind out of her. His chains and cuffs banged heavily against her, bruising and scraping her skin.

"Get off me!" she managed, gasping and grunting.

She tried to twist her ankle around his for leverage, but her foot got tangled in the chains running from his wrists to his ankle.

"I'm getting real tired of this," Logan said, breathing heavily.

"Then stop buying problems for yourself. All you had to do was sit on the couch and stay out of my way."

Logan rolled over and glared down at her. "Maybe I didn't want to sit."

The chains bit into her skin, his weight cut off most of her air. Her arms were pinned, one beneath her, one between. His hands were held low at his waist by the ankle chain pulled taut between their legs. Unless he moved, she was going nowhere.

"It beats getting shot, doesn't it?" She blew her hair out of her eyes. "I could have killed you."

A smile split his face. It was more feral than charming. "Yeah, but you didn't, did you?" He leaned closer. She bit down on a groan of pain. "I'm growing on you, aren't I?"

"Like a cancer," she bit out through clenched teeth.

"Where are the keys?"

She glared at him.

His smile faded. "Considering your current position, I'd say this now qualifies as 'need to know' information. I think I've made it clear what lengths I'm willing to go to."

Scottie opened her mouth to shoot a reply, then stopped. He had, in fact, made it clear, but not in the way he thought he had.

"You knew I wouldn't shoot you," she said. His stony stare confirmed it. "What kind of 'lengths' is that then?"

"Because you don't know that *I* won't shoot *you.*"

"All the more reason for me not to give up the keys."

"I don't think you understand the situation here."

"Oh, I'm real clear on the situation. You're the deluded one." She pushed a bit at his weight, grunting with the effort. "Damn, but you weigh a ton."

"It's the chains," he said pointedly.

No, it wasn't, she thought, remembering how he'd felt on top of her the previous day in the bedroom. She'd remembered that and many other moments, in excruciating detail, throughout a long, sleepless night. But when he'd settled between her legs that time, she'd—She switched off that mental rerun.

"Then I guess we're at a standstill," he said, tossing her words literally back in her face.

"You won't win this one, Logan."

"I've done pretty damn good so far."

She tilted her head just enough to run a pointed gaze over his chains, then back at him. "Oh yeah, you've done real well."

"I'm on top, aren't I?"

"For now."

"Face it, princess, you're having a hard time containing me." He grinned when she glowered at him. "Why don't we call it a draw now, before it gets embarrassing?"

She forced a saccharine smile, ignoring the sharp jabs of pain poking into her at every angle. "For who?"

He heaved an exaggerated sigh and settled his weight more heavily against her, cutting off all but a tiny fraction of what air she had left. "Well, I'm comfortable right here." He swung his head close, until his breath mingled with hers. "How 'bout you?"

Scottie swiftly reviewed her options. There weren't many, but it was difficult all the same. She tried to convince herself it was lack of oxygen to the brain, but the fact that she diverted her gaze from his told her otherwise. The man didn't fill space, he consumed it.

She pulled in what little air she could, adopted her best wounded pride expression, and lifted her gaze back to his. "Uncle." Her voice was a hoarse whisper. Nice touch, she thought.

"As in *The Man From*?"

Her palms itched to smack the smug smile from his face, but she maintained her strategically planned demeanor. "As in you win." Her scowl wasn't altogether feigned. "Bullies always do, right?"

His gaze narrowed. He studied her closely with obvious distrust. He was good. She was better. "No tricks," she lied. "I know a lost cause when I see one." She looked pointedly at him. "I gave it my best shot." She tried a shrug.

His wary expression remained. She waited, wondering if she'd overplayed it.

"What are you proposing?" he finally asked.

She tried to keep the victorious gleam from her eyes. "I'll unlock the damn chains."

"Just like that?"

"I wouldn't say having"—she struggled fruitlessly against him again, adding a pained gasp—"the life squeezed out of me by two tons of chained male is 'just like that.' I simply decided that you're right."

He raised his eyebrows.

She grunted and pushed at him again with her

knees. "And like you said, chained or not, with all this snow, you can't go anywhere. You're still where I need you to be."

"All true."

"So I'm not exactly losing. I consider it a compromise."

"If it makes you feel better, sure. It's a compromise."

"So, let me up and I'll get the keys."

Understanding dawned immediately on his face. He flashed a grin that was downright wicked. Her pulse rate responded accordingly.

"Ah, princess, you overestimate yourself. And you underestimate me."

"Believe what you want," she said blithely, hiding her concern. What in the devil could he have planned? "But if you want those chains off, you're going to have to let me go."

"Not necessarily."

Now it was her turn to be wary. Just who had laid the trap for whom? "What does that mean?"

"Well, as I see it, we have two options."

"Two?"

"Yep. One, we can crawl to wherever you stashed those keys together."

"Crawling might be a bit tricky with those chains. Of course, with your Magic Mel abilities, I'll give you the benefit of the doubt. But you'll still have to let me go to take them off."

"Who said *I* was going to unlock them?"

A good point. "What's the other option?"

He bent his head. What little breath she had caught in her throat. He didn't speak right away, letting the moment spin out as the tension—much of it frustratingly sexual—all but crackled between them, until she was convinced he could monitor her pulse rate and was waiting until it redlined.

"Option two," he murmured in her ear, "is that I make you tell me where they are."

"M-make me?" She damned herself for the edge her little stutter gave him. A man like him could turn an edge into a teetering cliff if she wasn't careful.

His lips brushed her neck. She gasped softly. "There are all kinds of . . . coercion." His voice was dark and silky smooth. Her body tightened. "Pleasure can be far more constructive than pain. Temptation instead of force. In fact," he added, teasing the shell of her ear, "I'm sort of hoping you hold out for a while."

"You sound quite sure of yourself." She, on the other hand, sounded quite shaky. Dammit, this was just what he wanted. *It's what* you *want*, her little voice whispered.

He grazed his lips along the column of her neck. "Fairly confident."

She shuddered, the sensation entirely pleasurable. *Stop him*, she commanded herself. Her body had already mutinied. But winning usually meant using brains over brawn.

Scottie shored up her resolve and turned her head toward him, bringing them nose-to-nose, almost mouth-to-mouth. "This plan could backfire on you."

"Willing to fight fire with fire, are you?"

His eyes were incredibly deep and dark. As close as she was, she couldn't distinguish between pupil and iris. They should have been cold, emotionless. They were anything but. They absorbed light, locked in heat. Inscrutable yet seductive, they mesmerized. She felt herself being pulled in, wondering what was behind those eyes of his. Dark secrets? Darker pleasures? Both?

"A worthy adversary you'll be, Scottie," he said, allowing a soft burr to color his words. He held her gaze. There was no mocking light there now. What she saw was challenge. Who would be the first to make a move? And would they move away . . . or closer?

Insanity. This was insanity. Even as she acknowledged the folly of the battle she'd somehow fallen into, she deliberately answered the challenge by letting her eyelids drift half shut and parting her lips slightly. Perhaps it was cowardly, wanting him to be the one to decide, especially when she knew what that decision was likely to be.

But her heart was pounding, her skin was alive with a thousand skittering sensations, all pooling inside her, creating an aching hunger, demanding to be fed. He'd chosen his weapon well. Temptation. He was the only man who'd ever been able to wield that weapon over her. She wondered if perhaps this particular duel had been lost before it had even begun.

His lips quirked as his gaze drifted lazily to her mouth. "You fight dirty."

Her mouth curved slightly at the corners. "I fight to win."

"Why is it I think we're both about to win?" He moved first, brushing noses, then tilting his head so his mouth would fit hers.

"This is insanity," she whispered, hardly aware she'd spoken out loud.

"Then lose your mind with me, Scottie."

The heat of his breath on her, with that electrifying

space between their lips spiked her hunger until it gnawed at her very soul. He had to be deliberately pushing her buttons, but her control was already thready at best and try as she might, she couldn't seem to form coherent thought much less battle strategy.

As she closed that tiny chasm she couldn't even remember what she was fighting for . . . or against.

She pressed her lips to his, but he was the one to groan. Winners? Losers? She didn't know. Didn't care. She only knew he was returning her kiss. Her entire being was centered in their joined lips. It was exquisite, erotic, that tight focus.

It was her turn to moan when he slanted his mouth across hers. He took her mouth almost lazily, as if he planned to defeat her defenses slowly and thoroughly.

She tugged at the hand trapped between them. She wanted to touch him as she tasted him. The need was enormous, but she couldn't pull free. His kiss was as weighty as his body. His tongue filled her mouth, and she let go of one need as she fixated on another. Slowly she twined her tongue along his, simultaneously fulfilling her twin desires of taste and touch in one delicious stroke.

He tasted . . . dark. It was the only word that struggled free of the mist her thoughts had become. Dark and deep. Oh the depths he pulled her to. His voice was a whisper of murmured need, urging her to continue. She did.

She tried to take him higher, faster, but he pressed her back, keeping to his slow, methodical plan of seduction. She should have been bothered by his tactics, but her senses were too saturated with pleasure and the worry slipped away on a sigh. The ache was still there.

The hunger increasing, not diminishing, with his every touch.

He slid his tongue from her mouth, pressed her lips closed with his, then ignored her moan of protest and worked his way over her lips again and again, giving and taking kisses that would be considered chaste if delivered by any other mouth but his.

She wanted to touch him. Badly. And worse was the need to feel more than his mouth on her. She wanted his hands touching her, she wanted his full weight upon her. She needed him to bury himself deeply inside her.

The ache centered and tightened into a vicious, demanding knot. Helpless to it, almost desperate to fulfill it, she arched her hips into his—and encountered the cruel reality of metal cuffs and steel chains.

She tore her mouth away, turning her head to the side to escape his continued assault. Panting heavily, finding air an almost impossible commodity, she struggled to remain calm, struggled to regain the equilibrium he had so thoroughly destroyed.

"Win or lose?" he queried hoarsely. The amusement threading his hoarse voice sharpened her senses a bit more quickly, yet she kept her head turned away until she knew she could face him with some semblance of control restored.

"The keys are still safe," she said finally, as she turned to look at him. Above flushed cheeks and well-kissed lips, his eyes danced like the devil's. She didn't want to think about what she looked like. "So I guess you lose."

"If you say so." He dropped a kiss on her nose before she could dodge it. She scowled even as her body jerked another knot inside her. His mouth curved into a slow smile that was almost more devastating than his kiss. "The keys are in your pack on top of the refrigerator."

He'd made the announcement calmly and confidently, but had there been a thread of doubt in him, she knew she'd blown it with her split second reaction.

Anger seeped in, along with a heavy dose of humiliation. "If you'd figured that out, then this . . . demonstration was for what purpose?"

He gave a little shrug. She wanted to wrap the chains around his thick neck and choke the smug light from those damnably knowing eyes.

"Fun?"

"We're not here to have fun, Blackstone."

"Well see, since you won't tell me exactly what it is we are doing here, I figure I'll fill the time whatever way I want." His voice slid into easy street dialect. "Whatsa matter, Scottie, don't you know how to appreciate a little fun?"

"In the right place, at the right time, sure." She wondered if he saw through that lie. She couldn't remember the last time she'd done something—any-thing—just for fun. Even if she had, she wasn't sure he qualified. Alternately irritating and mind-blowing, definitely, but fun? "I'm here to work, not play around."

"I don't know. I'd say you grasped the, uh, concept of play quite quickly. Maybe you need more practice." He started to lean toward her.

"Don't *even* think about it."

"Too late for that, princess. In fact, we've both done a whole lot more than think about it."

"And playtime is over." She stared at him, steely-eyed. "Move off of me. Now."

"Spoilsport."

"Now."

He started to move, then stopped himself. A grin spread across his face. "Good try there, Detective, but no dice. Deducing the location of the keys wasn't too difficult. But the original dilemma still stands."

He was right. Again. He wanted the chains off, but he had to get the keys and keep her captive at the same time.

"Mission impossible," she said with a hint of smugness.

"Nothing is impossible."

There were two guns on the floor. He had to let her go to get up. The instant he was off of her she could easily retrieve the one by the door before he could untangle himself and get upright. The other gun had tumbled from the table when it collapsed. The trick was she couldn't see it without turning her head. She had a better than fifty-fifty chance of getting her hands on it first. Would he go for those odds?

Even if he did get the gun first, he'd have a hard time retrieving the other gun or the keys without taking his eyes off her for a few seconds. Those chains severely limited his motion.

Climbing on a chair or even the counter would be all but impossible and even if he made that, reaching the bag would still be impossible. No way could he do that and keep her at gunpoint all at the same time. Unless—

She caught his gaze.

"Bingo," he said, nodding in approval. "Your mind works quick." At her mild look of surprise, he added, "You underestimate me, but I don't make the same mistake about you."

"I could refuse to climb up and get them."

"Then you'd have to make a choice."

"You can't lie on top of me forever."

His responding grin was unrepentant. She couldn't shut down the myriad of erotic images that flashed in her brain this time.

"Well, that is an argument we can have a little later," he said. "But that wasn't the choice I was referring to. You have to decide if you think I'll really shoot."

"I could reach the gun first," she reminded him. "I won't miss this time."

"I'll take my chances. So," he said, dropping his voice to a gravelly whisper, "you have to ask yourself, are you feeling lucky?"

Despite her very real dilemma, Scottie made a face. "Stick with *Star Trek*. Your Clint Eastwood is pathetic."

"Darn. There goes my career as a stand-up comic."

"Yes, well, bartending pays the bills I'm sure."

Like a light winking out, his eyes went flat. She'd thought they weren't cold? Goose bumps prickled her skin.

"You keep tossing my life in my face, Detective." He pushed closer, but this time there was only menace in the inky depths of his eyes. "Tell me, princess, what the hell do you really know about me?"

She knew he had an incredible talent for maintaining an insouciant air in the face of intimidating circumstances. She knew he was more skilled than any report on him was likely to reveal. She knew that if she was going to do her job effectively, she was going to have to push herself to the limits of her expertise and training just to stay a half step ahead of him. She knew that for the first time in her career, possibly in her life, she'd met her equal, if not her match.

And if she doubted that, all she had to do was remind herself that she also knew he could kiss like an angel and stir up fire like the devil and of how she'd come by that information.

"I know I don't think you'd kiss me like that then turn around and shoot me."

"You're sure?"

"Yes," she lied. She hoped, but she wasn't sure. "You're not the only one with deductive powers."

"And kissing makes me an unlikely killer?"

He'd done a lot more than kiss her, she wanted to say. Hadn't he? Or had the kiss that had unleashed such an intense rampage of emotion in her been nothing more than a pleasant diversion for him? She didn't know. Even allowing herself to think back over it, she didn't know. That was the one crucial piece of knowledge about him she didn't have.

She did, however, have another one. She held his gaze steadily. "No, it isn't the kiss that makes you an unlikely killer. Ted Bundy proved that. But the man who I saw in that bedroom at four o'clock yesterday morning was no killer."

His expression tightened, and his eyes, if possible, went even flatter. "You have no idea where you're going with that, and I'd advise you to stop now."

"I know a lot about you. What makes you think I don't know about Sarah?"

A muscle twitched in his cheek. "You asked me who she was. If you knew, you wouldn't have asked."

"Maybe I just asked to make you let me go. If you recall, it worked."

"Yeah, well I'm a fast study. I rarely make the same mistake twice."

Staring into his menacing expression, she thought of a third option. Now that he had figured out where the key was, there was nothing stopping him from just knocking her out, then doing as he pleased. She doubted he'd forgotten her chin jab.

As if he'd read her thoughts—and she was beginning to believe he had that skill as well—he said, "Better to cut my losses early for a change." His voice was like gravel once more, but it wasn't an imitation.

He started to shift on her, dragging his chained wrists upward. The intent in his eyes was clear, and it wasn't remotely seductive. There was no time to wonder just how far he'd go, and she couldn't risk being knocked out. She tugged her hand free and grabbed the front of his shirt. "Wait," she said.

His expression was cold. Deathly cold. Suddenly his irritating ability to make a joke out of everything didn't strike her as such a bad trait.

"What?"

"You can't hurt me. You'll never find out why I'm here. What I'm protecting you from."

"Oh, but I can hurt you. In fact, I could kill you and leave this place and almost damn well guarantee that no one would ever be able to prove it."

"There are at least half a dozen men who can put you in this cabin, on this date, with me, complete with documented proof. No, you won't get away with killing me."

She watched him assess the information he'd gotten from her. What she'd told him wouldn't compromise the mission. Killing or incapacitating her definitely would. She could not have him finding a way off this mountain and into the Brethren compound before New Year's Day.

"We both know I don't have to kill you to contain you," he said. "As to the other, you've made it clear you have no plans to tell me what you're really doing here, so that threat doesn't hold much weight." As he leaned in closer, the chains bit into her stomach. She worked hard not to flinch. "Or was that an offer?"

"What do you want to know?"

He laughed, and the hollow sound made her even colder. Who was this man? Not the one writhing in anguish and arousal on the bed. Not the one who'd kissed her into intoxication moments earlier. Certainly not the man who faced life-and-death situations with an impervious sense of humor.

What was he really capable of? She wished she knew who the hell Sarah was, and, more importantly, what had happened to her.

"I'll tell you what I can," she reiterated. If she could tell him just enough to make him let her go, she'd have a second chance at containing him. Of course, if she told him too much, she'd lose her value to him.

"Just like that, huh? I threaten you, and you cave. No force, no pain. I'm not buying it, Detective."

"Ask me a question. You judge if my answer is acceptable. What do you most want to know, Logan?"

A fleeting expression crossed his face, an emotion she couldn't—or didn't dare—put a name to. For just a second he'd looked . . . lost. A glimpse of need had flashed in his empty eyes. He swiftly, ruthlessly hid it, making her wonder if she'd imagined it. She hadn't. She couldn't have. Her life very well depended on it.

"Ask me," she repeated.

"What are you protecting me from?" He purposely rattled his chains. "Truth or consequences, Scottie. And I'm all out of patience."

How much to tell. Instinct battled with intelligence. Instinct won. "By keeping you here I'm protecting two people."

"Who's the other unfortunate bastard?"

"Your brother, Lucas."

SIX

Logan stilled. "What do you know about Lucas?" He'd assumed that she had to somehow be connected to his brother. It was the only reason she could have for tracking him down. But hearing someone else confirm that he had a brother unnerved him. No one knew of Blackie's deathbed confession but Logan and Blackie himself.

"I know quite a bit about him. We work for the same people."

He hadn't had much contact with the Brethren thus far, but from what he'd learned, he found it almost impossible to believe Scottie was one of them. For starters, she was female, and while there were women among the Brethren, as far as he could tell their main functions were to provide physical recreation, domestic help, and little else. "You don't exactly fit the profile," he said.

"For what? Who do you think he works for?"

Logan fell silent. She hadn't lied, he could see that. And she appeared willing to keep her word and tell him what she knew, at least to a point. Provided he asked the right questions. He was still suspicious. Just what did she know about Lucas? Whatever it was, she was willing to give up at least some of it in order to stay conscious.

"I'll ask the questions," he stated. "How do you know he's my brother?"

"That's an easy one. He looks just like you. A bit rougher perhaps, his hair is longer. Or it was the last time I saw him. But anyone with two eyes could see that you're twins."

So it was true. Really true. Blackie had told him where to start digging, and he had. His father had spent years looking for Lucas and had received serious information only a few months before he died. Logan had followed up on that lead, put his own contacts to discreet use, and had finally found him. Or at least discovered where he could be found. The day he'd gotten the confirmation that Lucas was indeed part of the Brethren cult had been both thrilling and devastating. He'd found his only living relative—his twin!—only to have already lost him to a bunch of manifesto-spouting lunatics. It seemed worse than cruel.

But cruel reality had visited him before.

Logan hadn't given up hope. His determination to at least see his brother, to talk to him, was unshakable. He owed it to Blackie, to Lucas, and to himself.

And now he'd met someone who had seen both brothers in the flesh, confirming in a way no one else could that Lucas Blackstone was indeed his identical twin brother. The same someone who could—would— make the meeting he so desperately wanted happen.

"When do you plan to see him again?" he asked.

"I honestly don't know."

"Scottie—"

"Listen," she said, cutting off his warning, "can we get up off the floor and discuss all this?"

"I don't think—"

"Tell me one thing," she broke in again. "Why do you want to find your brother?"

She stared him very hard in the eye, and Logan found he could only give her the truth. "Because he's all I have left."

She continued to study him for a moment, then released a small sigh. "Okay. We've both got cause to be here. You want to meet your brother, I know where he is. Why don't we cut out the cat-and-mouse games. I'll tell you as much as I can, enough to convince you to stay here for a week. I can promise a meeting with Lucas when this is over."

"And how do I know I can trust you?"

"You can't. But I'm the best deal you have right now to cut through a lot of hassle you still face in your quest to reunite with Lucas. I also know that if you don't do what I say, your brother's life and the lives of many others could be lost." Her steely-eyed gaze locked onto his. "Do we have a deal?"

"You'll take off the chains?"

"You'll promise to stay here and listen?"

Logan's grin was weary but felt good. He felt as if he'd gone fifteen rounds with Tyson. "Nothing's easy with you, is it?"

"Trust has to start somewhere," she said, a small smile of her own curving her lips.

He glanced just past her head and nodded. "What about all the play toys?"

Scottie arched her neck and glimpsed the gun. It was

less than a foot away. She looked back at Logan. "You knew it was there the whole time." He nodded. "I never had a chance."

He shook his head.

He watched her assimilate the ramifications, bemused by and impressed with how fast her mind worked.

"You still want to deal?" she asked.

His grin faded. "I want information about my brother. I don't want to hurt you to get it." He hadn't realized the truth of those words until he spoke them.

"Okay, then, I can work with that. As to the weaponry, well, we can either dismantle them and swap parts, rendering both guns useless, or we can act like big boys and girls and agree to play nice."

His grin returned. "I can be a big boy." Just like that, the ugly tension that had snapped between them vanished, only to be replaced by the all-too-familiar tension he'd experienced earlier.

He wanted to trust her, but he didn't. Not yet. Logan knew he should stay on the straight and narrow. Keep a level head and proceed with caution. Sarah had taught him that.

But Scottie wasn't a play-it-safe kind of woman. Instinct had served him well thus far.

"I'll even make the first gesture of trust," he added. "Lie still," he ordered. She stiffened, but didn't move. "I can't use my hands for leverage, so you'll have to bear my weight for a moment. I'm going to roll off of you."

"And?"

"And the olive branch is that Glock by your head. It's yours. Keep it on me while you get the key. You can even retrieve the one by the wall, if it will make you feel better."

"You're sure?"

He held her gaze. "I know you have more dream-time drugs in that bag of yours and probably a dart gun to shoot it into me." He softened his voice. "No more needles, Scottie. That's the one thing I'll ask of you. Chain me, tie me up, shoot me if you have to. No more needles."

Scottie was shaken by the emotion he was working so hard to conceal. The request alone surprised her.

"Trust works both ways," he said.

"As far as I can tell, you're giving me all the weapons. What am I giving you?"

"Freedom and information. If it means meeting my brother, I'll give you all the weapons you want."

He was so sincere, it made her wary that he was setting her up. A man as well trained as Logan didn't hand over any advantage he didn't have to.

"Your mind amazes me, Detective."

Embarrassed at being caught ruminating, but determined not to show it, she said, "Meaning?"

"Always thinking, figuring odds, percentages, strategies. So careful to make sure nothing gets by you."

She could have mentioned how he'd managed to accomplish that feat rather handily, but she didn't bother. He knew it. "In my line of work, you can't afford to be any less than your most vigilant, because no matter how careful you are, things get by you. That's bad enough. There's no excuse for letting it be worse. But then, I imagine you understand that line of reasoning, don't you, Lieutenant Detective Blackstone?"

She'd wanted to prick him, but instead of dinging

his know-it-all arrogance, her verbal spear had hit somewhere much deeper than a surface attitude.

"Yeah, I know that one real well." His eyes went flat once more, his expression closed up tight. "You ready? Brace yourself and I'll try and roll off as quickly and gently as I can."

Scottie put her free hand on his arm. "Logan, I—"

"You want me off of you or not?" He all but growled in her face.

Her urge to apologize vanished. It was just as well. Intimacy and Logan Blackstone had already proven a far too volatile combination. Her own expression steely, she said, "Sure. Go for it."

There was a brief flicker of something—remorse?—in his eyes, but the sudden bite of the chains chased it away. It was over in less than five seconds, but that didn't make it feel any better.

Scottie immediately reached for the Glock, groaning as blood flowed back into the arm that had been pinned beneath her the entire time. "You know, if you ever lose your job as a bartender, I'm sure you could get one as a steamroller."

Logan said nothing. He'd rolled to a sitting position and was untangling his chains, ignoring her and the weapon she now held.

There was a pang in her chest that felt suspiciously like regret. He's business, not pleasure, she reminded herself. She swallowed a groan as she slowly crawled to a stand, unable to tear her gaze away from the humbling sight he made. Even chained he'd been nothing less than magnificent.

"Can we hurry it up here?" He didn't look up from his task.

Scottie stilled for a moment, surprised by his surly tone, then shook her head, angry at herself for being stupid enough to waste even a second feeling sorry for him. She'd do well to remember the caliber of man she was dealing with. She ignored the part about how that caliber extended to his talent for kissing. Instead of laying the Glock on the table as she'd been about to do, she stubbornly shoved the gun in her waistband.

"Yes, sir. Right away, sir." She didn't bother tempering her sarcasm. She was, after all, holding the gun. That reminded her. She crossed the room and scooped up the second gun.

"The keys?"

She made a face at his back, then righted one of the chairs and dragged it to the refrigerator. She climbed up and reached for her gear bag. "You know, for someone who gave away all his toys, you sure aren't playing very nicely." From her vantage point, she looked down at him. That was when she saw the blood.

She hopped down, shoved the bag on the counter, and crossed the room, dropping to her knees beside him. "What did you do to yourself?" She started to reach out to touch his wrists where they had been carved up by the handcuffs, but he raised his head and froze her with a black stare.

"*I* didn't do anything."

"*I* didn't make you clasp them so tightly," she responded evenly. "Let me look at them."

He started to speak, but bit off whatever he'd been about to say. Probably just as well, she thought. He released a short sigh and in a quieter voice said, "It's no big deal. If you want to help me, get the keys and take these things off."

His quiet appeal motivated her more than a dozen demands would have. Without another word, she retrieved the keys along with a small first-aid kit, then crossed back over and squatted down in front of him.

"Ankle chains have to come off first," she said. She didn't look at him as she carefully lifted the chain and unlooped it from his handcuffs. When he lifted his wrists for her to unlock the cuffs she saw they were more scraped than cut, nothing serious, but she hated it anyway. Visions of him lying sprawled across the white linen sheets in all his leonine perfection flooded her mind.

Ridiculous as it was, she felt as if she'd desecrated a valuable piece of art, but the real wound was far worse than a superficial scrape. Avoiding his gaze, not daring to risk just what he'd see in her eyes, she very carefully sprung the lock. The metal bracelets loosened immediately. He pulled his hands back and let the handcuffs drop to the floor.

He didn't move right away or say anything. The silence deepened, becoming awkward. Scottie opened the first-aid kit, then she raised her gaze to his face.

He was angled away from her, massaging his thighs and calves. For all the war games that had gone on between them during his brief captivity, this quiet resolution should have felt somewhat anticlimactic. It didn't.

Tension simmered and hummed just below the surface. She imagined she could feel it bubbling along inside her veins, stirring things up, pushing her, prodding her, until she—

"Turn around so I can clean those up," she said, a bit more crisply than intended.

"It's nothing that won't clean up in the sink. Trust me, I've been much worse off."

He was right. She knew that, knew he'd been a street cop, knew he'd probably been scarred more than once in his past line of work. "Not by my hand you haven't."

He turned then. "You're in the wrong profession if drawing a little blood bothers you, Detective."

"Trust me, I've done far worse."

He nodded, conceding the point.

Maybe it was because he'd accepted it as fact too readily, but she felt compelled to clarify, though heaven knew why his opinion was so important to her. After all, she had drugged, shot at, and chained the man within twenty-four hours of meeting him. Why the hell shouldn't he believe her capable of worse?

"I'm more than willing to do what I have to in order to get the job done," she said, "but never without due cause or provocation." Her tone turned dry. "Not that you didn't do your best to provoke me." The remembered sight of him hunched over, untangling his chains, blood running down his wrists made her dip her chin. "But then, in your position, who wouldn't have?"

"Boy, are you always so conflicted over your work?"

She looked up, surprised at the return of the mocking note in his voice. It was the first hint of the "old" Logan Blackstone she'd heard in what felt like hours. It was alarming how deep the rush of relief went. Even more alarming was the unique sense of camaraderie she felt with him. She'd never had more than a surface sense of teamwork with her fellow Dirty Dozen agents. They'd have given up their lives for one another, but only in order to get the job done, not as a personal, buddy-for-a-buddy sacrifice.

She'd certainly never felt this . . . kinship of spirit. Not with any of her fellow cops when she'd been on the force. Certainly not with her father or her husband.

Confused, she forced her honest smile into a polite one. Business, she told herself, he was business. She'd sort the rest out later.

"I get the job done," she said with equanimity. "The ends always justify the means, but that doesn't mean I always have to like it."

The light sparked again in his eyes. She hadn't realized just how flat they'd become until now. Until she'd said something to regain his full attention. She turned *her* full attention to the first-aid kit. She'd wanted the kidding, teasing Logan back. Only now did she realize it made no difference which side of Logan Blackstone she was seeing, they all confused her on some level, made her feel things she couldn't identify, classify, sort, and file away.

"And here I thought you admired my end."

Her smile played a tug-of-war with her frown, edging out a victory at the last possible second.

"Among other things," he added.

She rolled her eyes, relying on sarcasm to create at least a thin shield. "Whatever makes you feel better." She handed him the kit. "Here, clean yourself up at the sink and I'll get what's left of the table scraped into a pile."

Surprising her, he took the kit without comment or complaint. He was at the sink, rinsing his wrists when he spoke again. "Do you always do that?"

"What, clean up my messes?"

"Cut and run when you get the least bit confused by something you don't immediately understand."

She stilled for a telling moment, then went back to picking up the splintered shafts of wood. He didn't miss anything. She remained silent, knowing anything she said would only prove his point.

"That surprises me," he went on. "You don't strike me as a coward."

He'd pushed the wrong button. "A coward?" she said, her tone both incredulous and defensive.

She didn't strike *any*one as a coward. That was a promise she'd made to herself the day her husband and father had died. Not before or since had one person ever looked beyond her competent, confident, no-bull exterior and questioned what lay beneath it. No one ever questioned what made her who she was. She'd taken the job with Del to insure no one ever would. She'd been very successful. So successful, she'd almost forgotten what lay beneath herself. Until now. Until Logan.

"Prudent, strategic, well thought out," she countered, working a bit too hard to keep her jaw relaxed. "That's how my actions are usually described." She held his steady regard without blinking, purposely meeting the challenge head-on. No one would ever suspect she questioned the outcome. "Along with fearless, commanding, and successful."

He was drying his hands and wrists carefully, but he held her gaze with total concentration. He stared at her just long enough to make her wonder exactly how far under the surface he could see.

Then he blinked and the intensity vanished. He lifted one shoulder in a half shrug. "Whatever makes you feel better." He turned back to the counter and laid the hand towel out to dry.

Scottie remained frozen in place. It was as if he'd flipped a light switch off. One second the entire room crackled with awareness and he looked at her in a way that made it seem as if he could decipher her genetic code if he chose to. An instant later he was casually tossing her words back in her face, then turning away as if he were unaware he'd been plucking out pieces of her soul in the process.

She didn't buy it. "Now who's cutting losses and choosing not to understand?" *Let's see how* you *like being analyzed.* "You don't strike me as a coward either."

"We're all afraid, Scottie. Even you. Some of us just do a better job of confronting and managing the fear." He leaned back against the counter and crossed his arms and his ankles.

He'd surprised her yet again. His tone had been neither casual nor patronizing. It had been . . . inviting.

"So you're saying I have poor management?"

He pushed away from the counter and walked slowly toward her. "No. I'm saying that it's not just about getting the job done. It's not just about bulling forward no matter what. Sure that makes you look bold and daring." He stopped right in front of her. "But it doesn't mean you're not a coward."

From her position she had to look up in order to maintain eye contact. The supplicant pose was not lost on her.

"You can't just *manage* what scares you," he said. "That's just finding a way to shelve it so you can move around it. That might get the job done, but it doesn't make you stronger. You have to confront what you fear, make yourself analyze it, break it down, figure out the why of it. Only then can you figure out how you're going to deal with it."

He was impossibly big, impossibly imposing, and completely intimidating. Yet she wanted nothing more than to pull herself upright and tuck her body against his, put her cheek against his chest and seek out things like solace, shelter . . . peace.

"And what if my way of 'dealing with it' is to shelve it?" she asked, proud of her steady voice. Inside she was panicking big time. He was right. In order to be truly strong, she had to face what confused her. She'd always known that. But for ten years, she'd been able to get away with ignoring that fact.

Unfortunately, what confused her most was Logan himself. She was certain she could ignore his challenge and do her job effectively. All her instincts were screaming at her to take the safe path her job always provided. Yet, she had the strong sense of foreboding that if she ducked around it this time, she might regret it for the rest of her life. A hell of a decision.

"Then you're not really dealing with it all." He crouched down, putting himself eye level with her. "Are you?"

He took up way too much space. Certainly more than was physically possible. Scottie felt trapped, cornered, overwhelmed. Not by Logan, but by the threat he posed. The challenge he presented. On all levels.

Stay and face it, she told herself. She looked into his eyes and knew. Facing him would entail much more than dealing with what he made her feel, what he made her want, that he had made her want at all. She wouldn't be able to face the deep-down parts of her he was affecting, without dredging it all up. All of it.

All the confusing questions and concerns that had plagued her two nights before rose again like a haunting specter. That's what this was about, she decided, grasping desperately at the explanation. It was all that moody, uncharacteristic introspection before Del's call that was making her react to him this way.

She didn't have to face it.

It had nothing to do with strength or cowardice, and she didn't give a damn what he thought. *Liar*, her mind whispered. Scottie ignored it, scrambled backward, and pushed to a stand, brushing off her pants. Logan didn't move. Logan was now in the supplicant position.

Funny, but she didn't feel even remotely that she controlled him, much less dominated him. Even chained, he hadn't let her do that.

He shifted up onto his knees and looked up at her. "Don't run, Scottie."

She stood there, frozen in indecision. It was a unique and terrifying sensation she'd like never to repeat. Her instincts told her to run. If she couldn't trust them, what could she trust?

"Will you answer one question?"

She simply stared at him.

He waited a beat, then said, "I'll take that as a yes." His humor didn't shake her from her almost trancelike state. She felt as if she were at a crossroads of some kind, and it was critical to the rest of her life to choose the right path. Wrong decisions couldn't be taken back.

"What are you really afraid of, Scottie?"

She looked at him, really looked at him, and spoke the words that had immediately come to mind. Words not born of instinct, but from her heart. "I'm afraid I'll make the wrong choice."

The moment she spoke she wished she hadn't. Hearts couldn't be trusted. That was the first thing she'd learned in life, the initial lesson taught by her father. Jim had been her graduate course in the subject.

"And what are you afraid is going to happen to you if you do?"

"I'll lose control." Again, the words were out before she could stop them, as if a strange compulsion had overtaken her, one she couldn't deny.

Logan reached out his hands. He'd rolled up the sleeves of his shirt so they wouldn't rub the abrasions and cuts around his wrists. Scottie fixated on those newly forming scars. Causing them was what had led her to this discussion, brought her to the actual crossroads. *He* was the compulsion. He was the one giving a voice to her heart.

And she knew why. He was the first person to understand she had one. She'd never been more terrified in her entire life.

"I don't want to do this," she said.

"Oh, I think you're dying to do this." He continued before she could protest. "I think you've hit the point where you can't not do this."

"What makes you the expert on what I need to do or not do?"

"Experience," he said simply. But they both knew it was so very complicated. "I've been right where you are. Different decisions, different reasons for making them, but the same fear motivating them. Loss of control. In other words, trust."

She didn't know how to respond. His assessment wasn't just uncomfortably close to home, it was a direct hit. It made her want to run fast and hide deep. That was the easy part. She'd done that many times. There was comfort in that routine. Safety.

At least that was what she'd always thought before.

He also made her want to open up, to spill all the anger and confusion and pain she'd kept locked up inside, release herself from the bonds of anguish she'd thought she'd been successful at dominating, when in fact those bonds had dominated every aspect of her life all along. He'd understand. She could tell him.

There she could find the possibility of real comfort. Of true peace. Safely delivered once and for all from the demons of her past.

"How long have you been in your present job?"

The question took her by surprise, jerking her from her thoughts. She answered without thinking. "Ten years."

He made a quick visual assessment. "Then you must have gone right from the force, or soon thereafter."

"What does that have to do with anything?"

"Why did you leave the force, Scottie?"

And like the snap of two fingers, the haze of confusion abruptly cleared. Righteous anger took its place. *So much easier this way*, her mind taunted. *Shut up*.

She glared at him. "You're good, Blackstone. Damn good."

Now it was his turn to look confused. His hands dropped back to his sides as he stood. "What in the hell are you talking about?"

She folded her arms. "Where did you learn that interrogation technique, certainly not with the Detroit PD?"

Now *his* face clouded with anger. He planted his hands on his hips. "Is there anything you *don't* know about me? Why is my past so damn important to you? What does it have to do with Lucas?"

Scottie dipped her chin and bit her bottom lip. She hated the sense of betrayal she felt. It was another emotion he shouldn't have been able to rouse in her. It was her own damn fault, trusting her heart. She knew better, dammit. She knew better.

Logan closed the distance between them and gripped her shoulders. "Answer me!"

Acting purely on reflex, Scottie whipped the Glock from her waistband and pressed the barrel under his chin. When rational thought kicked in, she decided to leave it there.

"Isn't that what you wanted anyway? Answers?" She nudged the barrel, forcing his chin up. "Wasn't that the point of that whole 'let's help Scottie with her fears' psychobabble exercise?"

"I'm not the one babbling here," he said with annoying equanimity.

With a sigh of disgust, she jerked the gun away and holstered it again in the back of her waistband. "Men. Can't talk to 'em, can't shoot 'em." She started to stalk off, but he grabbed her arm, swinging her back to him. Caught off balance, she moved heavily against him. She pressed her hands against his chest, only to be caught in a tight embrace.

"I don't know what set you off running again, but I wasn't pulling some elaborate scam on you to get information."

She tried to push away but his arms only banded tighter around her. She refused to admit, even to herself—especially to herself—that being held in his arms, even in a restrictive manner, was better than she'd imagined. She pushed harder.

He didn't budge an inch. "Look at me."

Scottie mutinously stared at his chest.

"What, you can't even meet that challenge?"

Her gaze flew to his. "Don't even start!"

He smiled. "Worked, didn't it?"

"Go to hell."

"I think I'm the one being conned here."

"What are you talking about?"

"You go to some pretty amazing extremes to convince yourself you're right to run."

She pointedly turned her head away, refusing to look at him. "I'm not going there again."

He shifted her against him and freed a hand. Still holding her snug to his side, he cupped the back of her neck. "You'll tell me about Lucas." His voice was quiet, but there was steely determination in his eyes. "But not until we finish the conversation we started here a minute ago."

SEVEN

Logan had finally lost his mind. It was the only rational explanation for what he was doing. Of course, if he was insane, it would be impossible for him to know what was rational and what wasn't.

Scottie had his mind running in so many directions, he hardly knew which lead to follow anymore.

"You want to talk about Lucas," she said stubbornly. "Then let's sit down and talk."

Logan switched tactics. "What's your hurry all of a sudden? You're the one who said we can't go anywhere? We have plenty of time for both."

"Well, you'll have to excuse me then, I'm not in the mood for a psychotherapy session right now. Perhaps later."

He wanted to smile, but knew it would be a big mistake. This whole thing was a big mistake. He did want to know about Lucas. Problem was, he was just as tantalized by finding out about Scottie. She'd drugged him, chained him, shot at him, tied him naked to a bed, refused to tell him why, then kissed him as if she'd never known what a kiss was before his. She fascinated him, monopolized his thoughts, skewed his perspective, and made him want her. Badly. He'd never been so intrigued and captivated by one woman. There was a twinge near his heart. Not even by Sarah.

As part of his mind insisted he drop it and focus on finding out about Lucas, another part had him saying, "You and I both know damn well there won't be a later."

She leveled a deadly look at him. "Oh well. Deal with it."

Didn't she know that the more she resisted, the more determined he became? And then it hit him, why he was being so doggedly persistent, why he couldn't shake this fascination he had with her. It went far beyond matching wits and mind-blowing kisses. In her, he sensed a kindred soul.

Hadn't he just told her he understood her need to run because of the years he'd spent running? His wanting to make her open up and face things wasn't an entirely altruistic gesture. Had something inside him sensed that if he could prod her down that path, he could follow? Join her? Finally face his own demons? Then neither of them would have to do it alone.

Alone. The word rang in his head like a death knell.

Isn't that what he'd really been running from in his tenacious search for his brother? His single-minded pursuit had been fueled by far more than a deathbed confession. It had been fueled by fear. Fear of being finally and eternally alone.

Logan felt himself getting pulled deeper and deeper

into the dark morass of his own troubled mind. The urge was strong to turn away, to shelve it . . . to run.

He looked down at Scottie's stubborn countenance. Oh yes, they were kindred souls all right.

She didn't want to face her demons, neither did he. Who was he to push her?

He dropped his arms and stepped away. "Fine, okay." He walked over and sat down on the small, beat-up couch. The springs gave easily, even the throw cover tossed over it was worn and faded. He gestured to their surroundings. "Wonderful ambience, don't you think? Why is it that hunters feel they have to live like Spartans? Does it make them feel more predatory or something? Me, I prefer all the amenities when I travel, otherwise, what's the point?" He looked back to Scottie, careful to keep his expression open and sincere. "What do you think?"

She still stood by the ruins of the decimated table, facing half away from him, exactly as he'd left her. He settled back into the couch.

To her credit she didn't look at him as if he were a complete lunatic. She looked at him as if she were completely aware of what he was doing.

"Why the sudden change of heart?" she asked.

"For someone who is so doggedly determined not to talk about herself, why are you looking a gift horse in the mouth?"

She cocked one brow. "Oh, is that the part of the horse I'm looking at?"

He laughed. "Sharp. Very sharp." He clapped his hands together. "So, you want to talk shop first or get something to eat?"

She eyed him warily. "I told you. I don't cook."

"I think I figured that out." He stood.

She watched him walk past her to the tiny kitchen. He felt her studying him, trying to figure out what he was pulling now. He could almost hear the wheels turning in her mind as she sorted, analyzed, filed, and planned. She was as relieved as he was to let the conversation change course, but she didn't like it that he had been the one to steer it in that direction. It made her suspicious, distrusting.

He smiled to himself. He understood her too well. As well as he understood himself.

"You want eggs, bacon, and toast?" He lifted one from the array of boxes she'd lined up on the counter. "Or another one of these yummy power bars?" He turned the box over and pretended to read the ingredients. "Just what I thought. Compressed sawdust and tree bark, mixed with healthy, wholesome chemical additives. Mmmm."

He looked up just in time to catch her stifling a smile of her own. A little buzz lit over his skin. He discovered he really liked making her smile.

He nodded toward the cache of boxes. "What, you own stock in the company or something? Don't you get tired of the same old thing?"

She stepped closer and took the box from his hand. "They're easy, efficient."

"Just the way you like things to be."

She didn't rise to the bait. He discovered he enjoyed that too. No easy scores with Scottie.

She moved past him and stored the box back on the counter. "I happen to like them."

"So, no eggs for you?"

She turned and shot him a fast grin that would have

blown his socks off, had he been wearing any. "If someone else is cooking, that seems pretty easy and efficient to me." She grabbed her gear bag and headed toward the only bathroom. "I take mine scrambled. With a little cheese, if you have it. Butter on the toast, no jelly. Two pieces."

Logan grinned broadly at her back, but soberly asked, "What, no bacon?"

She paused at the door, eyebrows raised in mock horror. "And ingest all those nasty chemical preservatives?" She went in and closed the door. A moment later, he heard, "Three pieces. Crispy, not burned."

He shook his head, chuckling. To himself, he said, "You are a piece of work, Scottie whatever-your-last-name-is." That, he decided right then and there, would be the first thing he'd find out. "Are you always so bossy?" he said so she could hear him.

Over running water, he heard, "That's why they pay me the big bucks."

"And who would 'they' be?"

"You never quit, do you, Blackstone?"

"That's why they don't pay me the big bucks."

He heard her chuckle.

He discovered he liked making her laugh too. It spurred his mind down the path of all the other things he might enjoy making her do. Grinning, he started breakfast, lighting the propane cookstove he'd brought with him. The cabin had electricity which ran from a generator, but he'd learned the hard way that it wasn't always reliable. He didn't push his luck past relying on it to keep the refrigerator cold and his brief showers hot. He had the bacon on and the bread on the rack toasting when he realized he was humming. Actually humming.

He paused in his work. Logan Blackstone was not a hummer.

He thought about it for a moment, cast a glance at the closed bathroom door, found himself spontaneously grinning at the thought of going the next round with the woman who was presently behind it, then turned back to his work . . . and his humming.

The tune his subconscious had picked out amused him. "Anticipation."

Scottie sat on the closed lid of the toilet. She could hear Logan moving around the cabin, her stomach was responding noisily to the delectable scents that curled under the closed door. If the food tasted a fraction as good as it smelled, she'd have to find a way to insure he cooked all their meals.

Well, isn't this cozy, she thought, with a self-deprecating smile. Not fifteen minutes earlier she'd had the barrel of a gun jammed beneath the guy's chin and now, there she was, happily fantasizing about his cooking skills. Before she knew it, he'd have her wanting to make curtains from old bedspreads and put dried flowers on the table.

Except they'd broken the table. Right before he'd kissed her. Right before she'd kissed him back.

She dropped her forehead into the palm of her hand. "God, what a mess I've made of this." Del would be checking in by noon. He would know something was up. She had to have the situation under control before she gave her report, or there was no telling what the repercussions would be.

She gave a humorless laugh even as her stomach

growled again. Repercussions to what? Her career?
Now that Del had revealed his continued involvement
with the team, she had no idea exactly what her role was
anymore. Would she still run the team? Would he expect her to return to the field? Did that idea bother her?

"What the hell difference will it make if it bothers
me or not," she grumbled. "After this debacle, I may
not have to worry about making that choice."

A sudden rapping on the door had her leaping off
the seat, hand immediately on her weapon.

"Who you talking to in there? If it's just yourself,
then come out and talk to me. Sounds like I'm in a
better mood."

Heart pounding, she silently growled at the door as
she relaxed and let her hand drop back to her side.

"Back off, Blackstone."

"Boy, good thing I made coffee."

"I hate coffee." She didn't, but she felt like fighting.
She wanted to be mad at him, but she wasn't. She
wanted to think of him as a citizen under her protection,
even a subject under interrogation, or better yet a crimi-
nal in her detention. None of those scenarios would
stick. What she kept coming back to was the unavoid-
able natural instinct to think of him as a partner, a team-
mate. She could not allow that to happen. She was an
avowed loner, both professionally and personally.

"If my scintillating personality doesn't tempt you,
perhaps breakfast will. It's ready when you are."

That was the crux of the whole problem. She would
never be ready where Logan Blackstone was concerned.

She wished she'd worked more closely with Lucas.
Perhaps it would have given her a better insight into
Logan. She and Lucas had occasionally been on the

same assignment, but rarely in the same capacity. Her specialty was mission control, his was infiltration, usually undercover. Not that identical twins were identical in thought as well as appearance, but right now she'd appreciate any help in dealing with Logan.

She opened the door and walked past him without looking at him. Avoidance was impossible in such a small cabin, but she needed any barrier she could erect. She carried her bag back and, for lack of a better place, stored it on top of the fridge.

There was no food on the counter. She turned as she said, "Where are we going to . . . ?" Her question died as she spied the faded throw from the couch. Logan had spread it on the floor between the couch and the woodstove. Their breakfast was laid out on a mismatched set of old plastic plates, framed by ancient flatware, slightly crinkled paper napkins, and recycled jelly jars posing as juice glasses. "Quite the spread," she managed, her throat strangely tight.

Logan stood at the edge of the blanket. "Yeah, well, one works with what one has."

It should have been nothing more than a warm meal on a makeshift table, a halfhearted picnic at best. But somehow Logan had managed to make it look charming and sweet. Thoughtful and . . . romantic.

Scottie's gaze was drawn past the blanket, to the broken table, and the handcuffs and leg irons and chain that lay just beyond. She felt heat color her cheeks. There was nothing the least bit romantic about this, and she was more the fool for allowing even a moment's fancy to color the scene otherwise.

"Thank you," she said, her tone brief but sincere. She crossed quickly to the blanket, wanting to eat her food and get back on track with the business at hand. It was a simple matter to discern which plate was hers. He liked his eggs over easy.

A flash of the scene from the day before crossed her mind. Had it only been little more than twenty-four hours since she'd first encountered Logan's naked, slumbering form, all twisted and tangled in those sheets? She heard his good-natured request for breakfast that morning echo again in her mind, coming after she'd drugged and restrained him to the bed. She let out a soft laugh of disbelief as she settled cross-legged in front of her plate. This was most definitely the last thing she had expected to be doing.

"What? You don't want the Tweety Bird glass?"

She glanced up at him. "I see you kept Taz for yourself."

"Typecasting?"

A raised eyebrow was her reply. His responding chuckle warmed her from the inside out. She grabbed the glass of orange juice and downed it as if that would extinguish the warm glow. So much for avoidance.

Small talk, she decided. They needed small talk to help establish some sort of base from which she could build a working relationship with this man. She searched for something inane to discuss, something to break the tug of tension that crept up between them at the oddest moments. *Like discussing cartoon character jelly jars?* She couldn't get much more inane than that.

"You're obviously not a hunter," she said, pushing ahead until a better plan presented itself.

"And you came to this conclusion how?" He'd settled himself catty-corner to her on the blanket. He seemed to take up way more room than she and the food did.

She struggled not to shift away. He'd notice.

"Amenities," she said, as if that explained everything. She realized she was staring when a slow smile spread across his face. She returned her attention to her plate. Small talk. "You like them, I mean. The conveniences. You don't like roughing it."

"And how did you come to that conclusion, Detective?"

She swallowed a bite of bacon before answering. She stifled a little moan of pleasure. "This is really good."

"Thank you. Now, you were commenting on my materialistic needs?"

"You said you didn't understand why hunters needed such Spartan living conditions. And you must be used to setting a better table than this, judging by your response to my compliment. So the obvious conclusion is you're no hunter." She scooped up another bite of eggs. How did he make them so fluffy on that little cookstove?

"Didn't they teach you not to jump to conclusions, Scottie?"

The way he said her name had her lifting her gaze to meet his, just as she pulled the fork from her mouth.

"Not all hunters are satisfied with only providing themselves with the mere basics," he said, his tone once again silky soft. "There are all sorts of prey to be had. Real predators don't stop until they get it all."

She paused in her chewing, her jaw locked, then worked to swallow the bit of eggs down her suddenly tight throat. He continued to look at her. He watched her chew, watched her swallow, then raised his intent look back to her eyes. The message seemed clear. He was marking his next prey.

Before she could make a decision on how to react, he shifted his attention back to his plate. When he glanced up again and caught her still staring, his easy smile had lost its predatory intensity.

She had really lost her edge, she decided. She was seeing things that weren't there. *Seeing what she wanted to see?* There was no denying the hot thrill that had stolen over her during their brief, but intense exchange. Her body certainly hadn't forgotten what it felt like to be pinned beneath his weight, her lips hadn't forgotten the taste of his mouth. What would it be like to be stalked by him? To be captured?

She thought she detected a knowing glimmer in his eyes and finally jerked her gaze from his. She bought another few seconds by munching down part of her toast. It was crunchy around the edges and soft in the center, where the butter had soaked in. Just the way she liked it. Food. Food was a safe place to start.

"I'll make you a deal." The instant the words were out, she realized she'd given him the perfect opening if he chose to continue his . . . hunt. She hurried on, purposely keeping her attention on her food. "I'll clean up and take care of the woodstove if you agree to take on permanent cooking duty. This is really incredible." She popped the last bit of toast in her mouth, then closed her eyes briefly as she swallowed.

"It didn't take much to seduce you away from those pieces of cardboard, did it?"

She smiled a bit dryly. "They're fast and easy, but even I admit they aren't the most delectable of meals. It wouldn't take much to seduce me." *Seduce me.* She caught the slight raising of one eyebrow out of the corner of her eye. Oh, yes he could seduce her. He didn't even need to cook. All he had to do was talk to her. Look at her the way he was right now. She cleared her throat. "Why don't we go ahead and get down to business."

He chuckled. "Anything you say."

She flushed. Freudian slip? She didn't think she wanted to know. She looked him in the eyes. "Let's talk about your brother."

The woman did know how to change the subject, Logan decided. He'd been quite enjoying her increasing discomfort. He'd quite enjoyed being the cause of the discomfort. What he hadn't anticipated was how much her reactions to his teasing would affect him. And she was affecting him. He was almost disappointed to change the subject—proof that he needed to jump off this train of thought right now.

Lucas. His brother. The only blood tie he had left. That was his purpose for being here. "You said you worked with him? When? For how long? For who?"

Scottie smiled. Logan thought she actually looked relieved. Don't get too relaxed, he wanted to tell her. *I'm not done with you yet.*

"Actually, he works for me now," she said. "We've been on the same team for ten years. The who is Uncle Sam."

"I didn't find any recent job description with Uncle Sam's name on it," Logan said, though he didn't disbelieve her. What had bothered him most during his background investigation of his brother was lack of *any* job description after he'd left the military. He knew that just because they were twin brothers didn't mean they'd have the same personalities or make similar career choices, but he'd still had a hard time accepting that his brother had gone from a stellar career in the army to a drifting globe-trotter with no apparent steady income.

Right now he'd be thrilled to death if she could prove that his brother was working for just about anybody else than a wacko cult group.

"My turn," she said. "Why have you only now begun the search for your brother?"

"You seem to know a great deal about me, Ms.—"

She hesitated a second. "Giardi."

He lifted a brow at the pause, but he was pretty certain she was telling the truth. She'd kept to her word so far. He'd expected he'd have to pull every bit of information out of her, but she was being surprisingly open. Of course, that, too, made him wary. "Ms. Giardi. Why don't you tell *me* why I'm only now looking for Lucas?"

She held his challenging gaze with far more equanimity now that they were talking business. He wondered if her discomfort when things got personal had to do with him specifically, or whether it was simply because she had a hard time dealing with anything that wasn't strictly job related.

"He doesn't know about you, Logan."

"That's not what I asked. But since you brought it up, how can you be certain?"

She finished off the last of her bacon with a decisive crunch. "It is imperative in our line of work to respect each other's privacy, but as his current commander, I can say with pretty strong conviction that he has no idea you exist. We didn't."

"Who's 'we' exactly?"

"My team," she answered smoothly. This time it was a dodge. He let her get away with it.

"You obviously know about me now, or you wouldn't be here interfering."

"Protecting."

"Yeah," he said dryly, "we'll get back to that in a moment. You said he doesn't know. Is that still the case?"

"Yes, it is."

Anger filtered back, mixing with all the other things she was making him feel. At least the anger was one emotion that didn't confuse him. "And you didn't think it was important to tell him about me?" He kept his tone steady, but he had no doubt she was reading his changing mood correctly. "Just how long were you going to wait? Or does it suit your imperative need to respect personal privacy to keep him in the dark?"

"Telling him hasn't been an option at this point. We only just found out about you."

"Well, 'we' must have been pretty damn disturbed by the information if they felt it necessary to send you out to climb a mountain after a heavy snowfall in order to 'protect' me."

"Concerned, not disturbed. I think it's wonderful that you want to reunite with your brother. I can't speak for Lucas, I don't know him all that well—"

"How in the hell can you work with a man for ten years and become his boss and not know him? Doesn't speak well for your managerial skills, Detective Giardi."

"Stop calling me that," she exploded suddenly. "Don't ever call me that!" Just as abruptly, she pulled herself together. He was as distracted by the sudden outburst as by her quick move to subvert it. He'd touched a nerve. A raw one from the looks of it.

"How our—my—team operates is something you couldn't understand," she said evenly. "Lucas spends most of his time in the field on assignments, some of them quite lengthy. I have no idea how he will react to discovering he has a brother, much less a twin. Even if we were the best of friends, it is unlikely I could categorically know that."

She'd continued as if her outburst had never happened, her tone smooth, unruffled. Only the slightly pinched skin at the corners of her eyes gave away the measure of what her control was costing her.

"So you think it's wonderful to see two long lost brothers reunited. Then why keep us apart? What is he really doing in that compound?"

There was another brief pause. He watched her wrestle with just how much to tell him. He hadn't meant what he'd said about her ability. He'd bet she was a very good commander. There was a firm, unshakable core of strength in her regarding her job—whatever that might be. But something was bothering her. Either personally, professionally, or both. He wasn't sure if her reaction to him earlier, to the kiss they'd shared, was the cause or just a symptom. And then there was the question of why the commander of the team had been sent and not another field agent like Lucas. He felt a rush of relief as he allowed himself to acknowledge that Lucas was apparently not a cult member, but an undercover agent for some covert government organization. His instincts about his twin had proved right after all.

"To protect you and Lucas, you have to stay apart for the time being," she said finally.

"From what? Who? Why is he here, Scottie? You said earlier that lives, his included, were at stake? Is he really in danger of being killed?"

"How much do you know about your brother? What specifically did you discover that led you here?"

Now it was Logan's turn to pause, to weigh his answer. She'd confirmed that his brother was really a government agent, but beyond that she hadn't really given him anything solid. He'd been just as subversive with his responses. Maybe it was time to tell her everything he knew. It was likely she knew it all already anyway, so he was risking little.

"Listen, why don't we cut the verbal Ping-Pong, here? You tell me everything you know about me, and I'll fill in the blank spots. If you're satisfied with that, then maybe you'll give me some straight answers about Lucas."

"I'm doing my best. I've already discussed more than I should have. I'll tell you what I can. I can't promise you more than that."

"I've waited thirty-seven years to meet my twin brother, and I'm not in the mood to wait any longer, so you'll have to give me a damn good reason to stay here for seven more days when I could be outta here in two or three."

"Try this one on then," she tossed back. "If you try and approach your brother before New Year's Day, you will not only probably get him killed, but you might go right along with him." She tossed her silverware on her plate, grabbed it and her juice glass, and stood. Glowering down at him, she added, "And if that's not enough for you, there are also a number of young children involved in this whole thing. Innocent children who will also die if you go blundering into a situation you know nothing about."

She made it to the small sink and had dumped the dishes in when she was spun around by a strong hand on her arm.

"Well, then why don't you explain this situation so that I do understand."

"I can't."

"Won't."

"The result is the same." She didn't shrink back from him, though he topped her above-average height by at least three inches. In fact, she braced her hands on his chest and pushed. "I'm sorry if you don't like it. But that doesn't change anything. You want to risk that I'm lying, then go right ahead. You'll be responsible for Lucas's death along with those sixteen children. Not that you'll have to lose any sleep over it since you'll likely get yourself killed in the process."

"You'd let me walk out of here?"

"Not without a fight I won't." His hand closed over the butt of her gun at the same time she reached for it.

"No more gunplay, Scottie." He yanked the gun loose, dismantled it, and tossed the parts on the counter where they landed with a clatter. She didn't flinch, nor had she taken her eyes off of him during his little demonstration.

He squashed the burgeoning respect he felt toward her. He needed anger right now. "We'll settle this, but not with bullets. More violence is not the answer."

She didn't soften either her stance or her tone of voice. "I'll sacrifice one life to save eighteen others if that's what you push me to. But I don't have to kill you to stop you. I get the job done, Logan. One way or another. Don't ever forget that."

"Then you better start talking. I'm not a fool, Scottie. I'm not exactly expecting the Brethren to open the door and invite me in for tea. I realize now that Lucas is not a cult member, that he's there for covert reasons. I'm thrilled as all hell to hear that, more than you can know, but if things are as dicey as you say, then I want to see my brother before he gets himself killed."

"I'm doing my best to make sure that doesn't happen, but you've got to play this my way. You've waited thirty-seven years, Logan. Give me five more days. You lose nothing but a little time. It's a small price to pay if it means lives could be saved."

He abruptly let go of her and stepped away. "Not true, Scottie. Sometimes a little more time can be the most priceless commodity in the world."

EIGHT

Scottie watched Logan stalk over to the sliding doors.

"Where are you going?"

He dug wool socks out of his duffel bag, tugged them on, then pulled on his boots, his back to her the entire time.

"Where can I go?" It was a rhetorical question, not a request for permission.

She answered him anyway. "Not very far, but out of here, I guess." *Away from me.*

He tightened his boot laces with a yank that should have snapped them off. "Pretty good deduction, Detective."

"I asked you not to call me that."

"Correction," he said, efficiently knotting his other laces. "You ordered me not to." He stood and faced her. "You should know something up front. I don't take orders real well. Since you've obviously had your hands all over my personnel file from the Detroit PD, I would have thought you knew that. Getting a little sloppy, Detective? Or should I call you commander?"

Scottie gritted her teeth and watched him walk to the sliding doors. He pulled on a black thermal ski sweater, the edges of his long green shirt hung out below.

He slid open the door. A rush of cold air blasted her clear across the room. She shivered but made no move to rub her arms. "When will you return?"

He looked over his shoulder. "What, no threat of shooting me? Don't you have tranq darts in your bag or something?"

"Like you said, where could you go?"

"You got up here."

"I had help."

"Which brings up another interesting question." He leaned in the open doorway, apparently impervious to the freezing slices of wind cutting through the room. "Why did I rate the commander of the team herself? Why not send a field agent up here to detain me? Shouldn't you be off somewhere running the show?"

It took considerable focus to stop shivering. However, now it was not only the cold wind threatening her. Logan was sharp. Scottie had given him far too much information, more than she'd realized, and he was putting it all together way too easily.

"The show is being run just fine," she said, keeping her jaw tight so her teeth wouldn't chatter.

"Just not by you."

Scottie didn't react. She didn't have to. Damn the man.

"We still have a lot to discuss," she said evenly.

Logan pinned her with his black eyes. There was

enough heat in that one look to keep her warm if she were standing naked in a blizzard.

"Yes, we do." He stepped out on the deck and pulled the door shut.

From where Scottie stood, she watched him cross the open area behind the cabin, heading toward the trees. His progress was slow in the thigh-high snow, but his determination was such that he seemed to wade through it like water.

Only when he disappeared into the trees did she think about following him. He wouldn't find the trail she'd forged. Even if she hadn't thoroughly disguised it, he was heading in the opposite direction. The timber was tall and closely packed. There was far less snowfall in the woods. But she knew that the stand ended less than five hundred feet upslope. And when he came out on the other side, the snow would likely be chest-deep. She spent another moment wondering if he was experienced enough not to end up over his head in the stuff. People died in much less snow, often within yards of shelter of some kind. She spent another moment wondering if her concern about his welfare was strictly job related.

The answer that immediately sprang to mind was not reassuring.

"He's too ornery to let something as flimsy as snow kill him," she muttered. He'd just glare at the snow, and it would melt a path for him. Still, she watched the tree line. Amazing, she thought, how one man could be such a mix of easy charm and deadly determination. The question echoed in her mind. *Just who are you, Logan Blackstone?*

"And why do I care so much?" she asked herself.

Scottie decided to use the break to do what she should have been doing all along—searching the entire cabin. Of course, the subject of her assignment was supposed to be restrained to a bed not traipsing about loose in the woods. She consoled herself with the fact that at least something was going according to plan. If she could turn up any information on Blackstone, preferably something that would support her "allowing" him his freedom, then she would be able to report something positive to Del when he contacted her.

She also hoped Del had something positive to report to her. She wanted more background information on Logan—such as where he'd been trained and what he'd been doing besides running a bar for the last five years. Maybe apples really didn't fall far from the tree. A fleeting thought of her father made her shudder, but she pushed past it and followed the original idea.

Had Logan ended up in espionage of some kind like his brother had? It would explain where he'd gotten the contacts to track down Lucas. Although it appeared now that even though he'd tracked his brother to the Brethren compound, he'd had no idea of Lucas's real reason for being in Montana.

She scanned the interior of the cabin. She'd already checked the bathroom. She thought about doing a more in-depth look in the kitchen, but her eyes strayed back to the other open door. The bedroom.

It was the best bet. She didn't waste time. She checked the armoire, but there was nothing hidden there. She checked under the bed, felt along under the slat supports. Nothing. She stripped the sheets off the bed, then pulled the mattress off. Nothing in the box springs. She ran her hands over all four sides of the mattress, scanning for any new seams or slits near the edging. Nothing. Then she noticed the manufacturer's label on the bottom, a big rectangular piece of printed silk. The adhesive used to adhere it to the mattress showed a bit more on one side than the other, as if the label had been peeled off and put back on slightly off center. She picked at one corner, then pulled it back.

"Bingo." Logan had cut away part of the bedding and made a small hidey-hole. She pulled out his wallet, a small envelope, another handgun, two ammunition clips, each fully loaded, and a passport. "Passport?" she murmured. To go to Montana?

She didn't have much time. The envelope and his wallet were the best bets for potential information, but curiosity had her picking up the passport. She flipped open the dark blue cover. There was a picture of Logan, taken at least a few years before. She glanced at the date of issue and saw that it was almost five years old. He looked dark and menacing in the photo, there was no hint of the easy smile and quick wit she knew he possessed.

She went to riffle through the pages, to see where he'd been in the last four and a half years, when her attention was caught by the name typed next to his picture. She'd been so busy checking dates, she hadn't thought to look. "Grant Hudson." The rest of the info on the cover page fit the man in the photo. All but the name.

There was no doubt he was Logan Blackstone—she had Lucas as biological evidence on that one—which meant Grant Hudson was an assumed identity. "Just a minor federal offense," she said sardonically. She glanced over her shoulder into the main area of the cabin. She could see beyond the deck from this angle. No sign of Logan. Still, she worked quickly. He'd been gone for over an hour, but even he wasn't tough enough to stay out in that much cold and snow with only boots and a sweater on for much longer.

She flipped through the pages of the passport. Almost every page bore entry or exit stamps. The countries represented spanned the globe, but she noticed that most were in the Middle East, a few more were from some of the newer countries that had formed since the demise of the USSR, and a few others were from Central and South America.

She flipped to the last page. The most recent date was less than one month earlier. Five weeks after his father had died. He was still active, so much so he took his passport with him even when on personal business. She considered the fact that he could be after his brother for professional reasons, but instinct based on his father dying so recently told her that wasn't the case. She closed the book, her mind already spinning as she dropped it back into the nest and picked up the envelope.

Why in the hell hadn't Del caught this information on his initial background sweep? She knew he'd been in a hurry because of the time frame, but with his contacts there was no excuse to let something that had so much potential to affect her assignment slip by unnoticed. Which meant Del had no clue whatsoever about Logan's alternate life. Which also meant that whatever team it was that Logan worked for was buried even deeper in the labyrinth of secret government agencies than the Dirty Dozen. A startling thought, especially when she knew that only a handful of people on the planet knew about the Dirty Dozen.

She dropped the envelope and quickly flipped open the wallet. Michigan driver's license. Picture, name, and address were all the same as the information Del had given her. She slipped out two credit cards, one gold, both inscribed with the name Logan Blackstone. There was a wad of cash, mostly twenties and fifties, in the billfold, about five hundred dollars give or take. She looked behind the driver's license and in every other slit and crevice, but there was nothing else in the wallet. She dropped it and unclasped the small manila envelope.

A driver's license, social security card, and a couple of credit cards slid out into her hand. All in the name of Grant Hudson. She slid them back in and pulled out a few folded pieces of paper. A photograph slipped from them to the floor. She picked it up. It was a part of a photograph, actually half of one. It was old, the black-and-white film fading to gray and yellow over the years. The picture was of a tall, well-built man with dark hair. He was wearing pleated pants and a white button-down shirt, and he was holding an infant. The smile on his face as he looked down at the child in his arms was very familiar.

"My father."

Scottie startled badly, barely squelching a scream. Logan was just behind her, looking over her shoulder. His cheeks were ruddy from the cold, and his hair was wind ruffled. It made him appear a bit wild, untamed. He looked more dangerous than ever.

"The . . . uh, the resemblance is uncanny," she said, scrambling to regain her equilibrium. There were very few ways to handle being caught red-handed. She opted for ignoring the crime and focusing on what the act had uncovered. "I take it the child is you?"

"No, he thinks it's Lucas."

Logan's expression hadn't changed, meaning he still had none. She had no idea what was going on behind those flat, black eyes of his. She doubted it was anything warm or positive.

"Thinks?" Keep him talking. She quietly stretched her fingers under the envelope until she could touch the gun. Just in case.

"According to my father this was taken about a month after we came home from the hospital. He's pretty sure he was holding Lucas, and my mother was holding me."

"Where's the other half of the photo? I assume it's of you and your mother?"

"I don't know where it is. Lucas could have it. This was the only photo taken of us as a whole family."

Something flickered in his eyes, but Scottie could only guess at the fleeting emotion she saw. Loss. Loneliness. Perhaps a combination of the two. Grief.

He suddenly became all too human to her; made vulnerable and threatened by past events he had no control over. She'd seen him like this one other time. When he was dreaming about Sarah. She now understood there was grief in that history too. She wanted to ask, wanted to help. He gave her the chance to do neither.

"My dad cut it in half when they split up. It was a couple months later. He gave the other half to her. A memento, I guess. I don't know if she even kept it."

She looked from the photo up to Logan. He towered over her, but suddenly she wasn't so afraid of him.

"But you're hoping Lucas has it. As some kind of proof?"

"I think just looking at him would be proof enough, don't you?"

She ignored his sarcasm. "Proof of family then. Proof of where you came from."

His dark expression shuttered further, but he said nothing.

"Do you know why they split up? Why they never told you about your brother? Or him about you?"

He held her gaze for what felt like an hour. She didn't think he would answer. Then he said flatly, "As a kid I was told she died. I don't know what really happened. My father didn't tell me until he was so far gone he could barely talk. He used what energy he had left trying to convince me to look for Lucas. Maybe he knows the truth."

"Did you really need convincing?"

"I was stunned. I was angry at him for lying to me all these years." He fell silent for a moment, his gaze unfocused, as if he were looking inward. She didn't break the silence.

"Later," he continued, his tone more subdued, "after he died, none of that mattered to me, all that mattered was finding my brother, which I would have done whether or not Blackie had begged me to."

Scottie could tell that it did still matter to him. He had a lot of unresolved feelings about what his father had done, and how he'd gone about trying to rectify it. It told her volumes that wouldn't be found in any report about how deeply Logan felt about his father.

Her own thoughts turned inward. "You were fortunate to have a parent who loved you that way and allowed you to love him back," she said quietly, not realizing she had given voice to her thoughts until the words were out.

Instead of inviting questions or further confidences, her comment seemed to jerk him out of his reverie. His expression hardened once again. "Find anything else interesting in there?" He nodded toward the hidden stash under her hands.

He made no move to bend down or interfere with her in any way, but she instinctively slid her fingers a little farther onto the gun handle. For those few moments she'd forgotten how they'd come to discuss the subject of his family.

It was clear he hadn't.

"Just your pretty basic wallet stuff. I didn't take any money," she added with what she hoped passed for a dry smile. "You can count it if you like."

He didn't respond to her attempt at levity. Instead he crouched down. She could feel the chill emanating from his clothes. It was the one emanating from his eyes that truly froze her in place.

"You got any other questions you want to ask me, Detective Commander?" His voice was black-silk slick and just as cold.

She worked hard to maintain even a semirelaxed posture. "I thought we'd already established that there are some things I'd like to know."

His gaze dropped directly to the passport, then cut back to her. The light that came into his eyes was faintly mocking. "Yeah, I just bet you do."

"Let me clean up here and we can talk in the living room." She didn't phrase it as an offer. Without waiting for a reply, she slipped the photo and papers back in the envelope. He had to have been spying on her long enough to know she hadn't seen what was on the papers. It was unlikely he'd show her now. She put the wallet and the envelope back in the hole on top of the gun and passport.

She pushed the mattress off her legs and moved to stand up, only to find herself unceremoniously hauled to her feet by a hand latched around her upper arm. She came up flush against him, tilting her head back in order to see his face, a face which presently appeared to be carved from granite. She found herself looking at his mouth and remembering his wide, easy grins. At the moment, it seemed almost impossible to believe he was capable of producing those grins, just as it seemed impossible to believe those lips had been intimately involved with her own.

"Keep looking at my mouth like that and I might get the wrong idea about why you want to talk to me."

His voice was a low vibration that made her shudder . . . and not with fear or revulsion. "I—" She tugged at her arm. It might as well have been trapped in a vise. "I . . . let me straighten the room up. Thanks for helping me get off the floor."

He continued as if he hadn't heard a word she'd said. "You know, talking is highly overrated. There are other, more effective ways to communicate."

She thought of the mattress lying literally at their feet. She remembered lying beneath him with broken shafts of wood poking her back and his chains digging into her stomach. Even then he'd "communicated" just fine.

"Communicating like—" She broke off and cleared

her suddenly tight throat. "Communicating like that would effectively end my career."

"Is your career in that much jeopardy?"

"Do you always seduce and interrogate at the same time?"

He surprised her with a soft laugh. "It worked for James Bond."

She pulled her head back and looked him in the eye. "Is that what you are, Logan? Or should I call you Grant?"

His smile remained, but the teasing light that had just returned to his eyes winked out. She shouldn't have regretted it.

"Cleanup time is over," he announced abruptly. Without warning he stepped over the pile of sheets, out the door, and yanked her along behind him. She barely kept herself from tripping over the corner of the mattress and had to hop over the linens.

By the time she regained her balance and could make a move designed to free herself, she found herself flung onto the couch. He hadn't done it harshly, but it earned him the expected result.

She rubbed her newly released arm and aimed a pointed look at him, but stayed where she was, watching him as he paced in front of the couch. "A simple, 'have a seat' would have been sufficient. If you recall, I was the one who suggested we talk. You were the one who suggested that we—"

He spun around, nailing her with a heated look the instant she stopped herself from finishing. "That we what, Scottie? Say it."

"Listen, we're two people, stuck in a cabin, there's a lot of tension and some of it's sexual. Okay, I admit it.

That's normal. It doesn't mean we have to do something about it."

He stopped and planted his hands on his hips. "I think it would beat the hell out of what we've been doing so far."

"Well, you'll have to pardon me if I don't strip naked and jump on you because it's more fun than doing my job."

The anger and frustration left his expression. All that remained was the heat. "As far as I can tell, your job is to make my life miserable for the next few days. So yes, I can damn well guarantee that it would be a whole lot more fun doing it my way." He stalked toward the couch. Scottie pushed back against the sagging cushions. What exactly was he planning to do? And did she want to stop him from doing it?

Her thoughts came to a halt when he stopped in front of her and bent over, placing his hands on the back of the couch, on either side of her shoulders. His face was now inches from hers. She'd spent a lot of time being close to him. For some reason this time was different from any of the others. Then she realized what it was.

This time he wasn't chained up.

"What is it you're really afraid of, Scottie? Losing your job? I don't think so." He dropped his gaze to her lips, then back to her eyes. "You know, there's more than one way to chain a man to a bed."

She swallowed, a difficult task on a suddenly dry throat.

"Hell, a few days might not even be enough. Mission would be accomplished, job saved. And we all know how important it is to you to get the job done, don't we, Scottie?"

Scottie scrambled to keep her thoughts focused. He'd asked what she was afraid of. It was a question she did not want to answer, not even to herself. Because it had nothing whatsoever to do with her career.

No, her fear centered on giving in to the thoughts, needs, and wants that had been plaguing her lately. Somehow they had all come together and were embodied by the man standing in front of her, offering her something she shouldn't take. She couldn't take. She wanted it too suddenly, too badly, too much. After half a lifetime spent never wanting at all, these feelings were confusing the hell out of her.

Whatever her reasons were for feeling this way about him and what he offered, they were certainly not the same reasons he had. Oddly, it was that conclusion that gave her the strength she needed.

"My mission will be accomplished anyway," she told him flatly. "My job and the eventual continuation of it are not your concern, or even mine at the moment. Right now I'm more interested in making sure that a dozen or so kids make it through next week with their lives. I'm interested in making sure your brother makes it out alive so he can be reunited with his twin. So back off and put your hormones away. There are things we have to talk about and none of them have to do with sex."

She held his level gaze, jaw locked, mouth firm. She had no idea how he would react, but the slow smile that eased across his face was not even on her list.

Liar, his eyes said. "I love it when you get superior, Commander."

Before she could pull away—she would have pulled away . . . wouldn't she?—he leaned down and brushed his lips against hers. "Stop all this running, Scottie, and kiss me."

"But—"

"Using kids as a shield." He gently tsked-tsked her and dropped another featherlight kiss on her lips. "Tugging heartstrings with visions of tearful reunions. You're getting desperate, Scottie. Running scared."

"Logan, we—"

"Nothing is going to happen to those kids or my brother for at least the next five minutes. Now, shut up and kiss me." He didn't let her argue. He sealed his mouth to hers instead. His kiss was gentle, coaxing, but, like the man himself, determined. He tasted warm, all aftereffects of his trip outside gone. Slowly, her own lips softened. She tuned out the cacophony of voices arguing in her head and for once, for blessedly once, just let herself feel. And enjoy.

He lifted his mouth the tiniest fraction. "Now sigh deeply and say 'Oh, James.' "

She stopped for an instant, knowing she should be affronted. But the teasing twinkle she'd missed was back in those dark eyes, encouraging her to relax and join the joke instead of making her the butt of one. She had to stifle the urge to laugh.

Instead, she did what he made her want to do, she joined him. She let her head loll back. Her eyes half closed, a lazy smile curving her lips, she exhaled long and deeply and in the breathiest, sex-kitten voice she could manage, she said, "Ohhhh, James." She drew the two words out, half-moaning at the end.

His eyes widened briefly. She'd surprised him with

that. Good. The curl of warmth that had formed deep inside her flared like a match to a candlewick. Playing with Logan was like playing with fire. The flames dazzled and beckoned. Once started, she found it too irresistible to stop. Another debate stormed into her head. Logan smiled. She tuned everything else out and danced a little closer to the fire.

"Latent Bond girl tendencies? I wouldn't have guessed." He dropped several small kisses along her bottom lip. "I think of you more like . . ." he drifted off, pondering while he plundered several more kisses from her now-pliant lips. She moaned, deep in her throat. He lifted his mouth and smiled. "Catwoman."

Secretly pleased with that analogy, Scottie smiled dryly and said, "Just another man with a latex fixation."

"Oh, it's not the catsuit that gets me." He nibbled along her neck. "It's that feline grace." He ran the tip of his tongue slowly along the outer shell of her ear. "The way she always lands on her feet." He nuzzled the hair behind her ear. "Nine lives can make a woman fearless."

Scottie was having a very hard time keeping track of the conversation. Most all of her attention was exclusively focused on keeping track of his lips on her skin. They were the tiniest of touches, bare tastes and caresses, yet he was wreaking the most delectable havoc with her central nervous system.

She tried to turn her head, to capture his mouth with hers. Her body was tight and achy. She needed more. His hand spanned her throat, long fingers curved over the edge of her jaw, keeping her neck bared to his mouth.

"How many lives do you have left, Scottie?"

She shuddered as his teeth pressed gently against her

skin. She felt him lower his weight to the couch, shifting her sideways, down, down. She raised her hand to find his, wanting, needing, to feel more than just his mouth on hers. She wanted him to touch her. Put his hands on her, run them over every aching inch of her. The need was beyond desperation, bordering on obsession.

"Touch me." The plea was little more than a ragged whisper. She didn't waste any time wondering how he'd brought her to this so quickly. Maybe she'd known this was what she wanted from that first moment she'd laid eyes on him, standing transfixed by the erotic sight he made, writhing in white linen sheets in the growing light of dawn.

Calling out another woman's name.

Scottie stilled, her hand stopped its seeking mission in midgrope. An instant later Logan stilled as well. All she could feel was his heart pounding against hers and his breath against her neck.

"What is it, Scottie?"

There was sincere concern in the gentle question. After their extended verbal parrying and thrusting, it wasn't what she would have expected from him. It was almost enough to make her shut out this final, more important argument and simply give in to her body's greater demands. Almost.

With his face buried against her neck and hers closeted in the dark sanctuary of his shoulder, she answered him. "Who is Sarah?"

She felt his breath catch. One moment passed, then another. Finally he let it out, a slow release accompanied by the relaxation of muscles that had suddenly gone tight at her request. That should have relieved her, instead it made her want to take the question back. Tell him she didn't really want to know. Save him from discussing something that would probably hurt him and very likely herself in the process.

"I loved her." It was a raw, gritty admission. It shouldn't have pierced her heart, but it did.

She took a moment to collect herself. He'd said "loved"—past tense. "What happened? Where is she?"

"She's dead." He lifted his head and looked at her. The anguish she saw in his eyes tore another jagged wound in her heart. "I killed her."

NINE

He'd never actually said the words out loud. Until now. Oh, everyone who knew him, knew he felt them, knew he believed them to be true. There wasn't an officer in the Detroit PD that didn't understand why he'd turned his badge in. Most disagreed with both the decision and the reasoning behind it, some quite vociferously, but they all understood it.

"I'm so sorry," Scottie said.

Pulled from his thoughts, he stared at her. Sorry? He'd just confessed to killing someone, and she was sorry for him?

"It's horrible when anyone dies," she went on. "No matter who he or she is, whether they're a victim or a villain. It's still a human being, lying there dead."

He just stared at her. She was looking at him, but he understood that slightly unfocused gaze. She was lost in her own thoughts, her own memories.

"But when it's someone you love . . ." Her voice

trailed off, then her gaze cleared and shifted to his. "I'm sorry."

"Yeah, losing someone is always hard. But she didn't just die, Scottie. I killed her. I was responsible." He was harsher than he'd meant to be, wanted to be, but for some reason seeing that look of understanding—true understanding—on her face had scared him. It was too much like being forced to look in a mirror. He didn't want to look that deeply into his soul. He didn't want her looking either.

Her eyes widened a bit. If there was a little hurt mixed in he ignored it. "How?"

The demand caught him off guard. "What?"

"How did you do it?" she asked, defiant. "Kill her, I mean?"

No one had ever asked him. Mostly because everyone who knew him knew how Sarah had died. But, he realized now, no one had ever forced him to talk about it either. Sure, there had been those who had tried to console him, tell him he was not to blame, but he'd shut them out, totally and completely. After a time, those who knew him understood he didn't discuss the topic. Ever.

That she had questioned him now, in such a cold, unflinching way, should have made him mad, should have made him want to lash out, should have made him rage at her for inflicting such pain.

Instead, he heard himself quietly say, "She was under my protection."

She didn't back down an inch. "What, you shot her by mistake or something?"

Anger flared, but he looked into those eyes, fearlessly challenging him, and he couldn't seem to grasp a steady hold on the emotion. "I didn't shoot her," he said evenly.

"Then tell me how you did it."

"Scottie, don't push—"

"I don't buy it."

"What don't you buy?" he exploded. "That I killed her? Or that I'm capable of killing?"

She looked him squarely in the eye. "You can kill. You have before."

"You should know, you've seen my service record."

But that wasn't it. There was a look of . . . knowing in her eyes, one that didn't come from studying his personnel file. This was the kind of look that could only come from experience.

"Who do you work for, Scottie?"

"Oh no, no table-turning."

"I didn't start this line of questioning. You expect me to spill my guts, so I'll ask anything I damn well please."

She paused for a moment, some of the defiance gone from her expression. "Do you want to stop?"

He opened his mouth to say yes—hell yes!—then closed it again. Did he? While it didn't feel good to talk about what had happened, much less his role in it, it did somehow feel . . . necessary.

He thought about the way Scottie had begun to respond to him. He could tell himself that his need for her was as basic as she'd made it seem. One man, one woman, one cabin, a ton of snow. But he'd be lying.

There had been some . . . thing, some tone, an honest need, lacing her request about Sarah, that he'd responded to on a level he didn't know he was still capable of connecting to.

"Yes, I want to stop." The light of battle winked out in her eyes, leaving only disappointment. Recriminations and accusations he could have deflected. But he discovered he was defenseless against disappointment in the eyes of Scottie Giardi. "But I'm not going to." He blew out a sigh and levered himself off of her. He settled into the other end of the couch, not sure where to look, much less where to begin.

She sat up slowly, tucking her feet under her. She ran a hand through her hair, using long, slender fingers to pull the tangled pieces free and smooth them down.

His attention was caught by the process, and he found himself wanting the responsibility for that task next time. Ridiculous. Where was this leading? He wasn't at all sure he wanted to find out.

"I'm sorry," she said, then raised a hand to stop him when he would have interrupted. "You're right. I really had no business asking about Sarah. It was just that I, that we—" She stopped and glanced down at her hands, now intertwined in her lap.

He didn't push. For once in his life, he didn't push.

She finally looked up. "I don't *do* this," she said as if that should explain everything.

Somehow, it did. "Scottie—"

"Let me finish." A brief smile curved her lips. "Just this once." The smile faded, and she glanced away, staring off across the cabin. "I'm not what you would call a casual person. I tend to take everything very seriously. And for most of my life, everything has been my job."

"You don't have to—"

Her gaze flashed to his. "Yes, I do. When I came into this cabin, my mind was on one thing and one thing only, preventing one Logan Blackstone from leaving the premises for the next few days. I wasn't expecting what I found."

He flashed a small smile of his own. "Had I known I was expecting company . . ." He was rewarded with another small curve of her lips, but that too slipped away.

"I've seen naked men. Even been naked myself with a few of 'em."

Logan was unprepared for the little spurt of emotion her dry statement elicited. It felt uncomfortably like jealousy. Or envy perhaps.

"But you—" She paused, then turned to look at him again. "You were magnificent. I thought you resembled some exquisite piece of art. Watching you move on that bed . . ." She blew out a soft sigh. "I was mesmerized. All thoughts of my job went poof!"

Her expression wasn't dreamy and ingenuous. It was as clear and specific as her words. Instead of pumping his ego, her honest description humbled him. He had no idea how to handle that.

"You still managed to get that needle in my backside."

"Barely. No pun intended," she added, another smile flirting with her full lips. "That's another example. Mistakes like that don't happen to me. You disconcert me. Professionally and personally. I think I've gotten a handle on the professional side, or the beginnings of one. There's a whole lot more to you than a cop-turned-bartender. But the other? How you affect me personally? Not a clue how to deal with that. I thought that letting go with you, giving in to what I wanted, was a professional battle, an ethical war between right and wrong as it applied to my job and getting that job done correctly. But it isn't about that at all."

"What is it about then?"

"It's just about me. It has nothing to do with my career or completing this assignment. It should be, but it's not."

"What about *you*, Scottie? What are you battling against?"

She laughed; it was hollow. "You probably think I'm a mental case at this point. All you want is a good roll on the couch and a way to keep from dealing with the situation for a while, and here I am doing a psychoanalysis—"

"What makes you think you're just a roll on the couch for me?"

That made her pause. It made him pause too. If she wasn't just a potentially incredible way to spend an afternoon or two, then what exactly was she? Good question, he thought. He wished he hadn't asked it. Sort of.

"I met you,"—she looked at her watch—"a little more than a day ago. What in the hell else could I be?"

"You tell me. It's been a little more than one day for both of us. What in the hell else could it be for you? You're the one saying you stopped for personal reasons. Is it simply that you're just not a roll-on-the-couch type?"

"See, that's just it. I'm not. But I would have been, could have been, with you."

"Except?"

She stared at him for a moment, then said, "Except when I walked into that bedroom at the crack of dawn yesterday morning, you were writhing on that bed in there, calling another woman's name. It shouldn't make any difference. It's just a fling we're talking about, right? I shouldn't care who she is, or what she meant to you."

"But you do." He understood. He thought about how he'd feel to hear her moan another man's name, and he was very afraid he understood completely. "And you had to know who she was before you could . . . roll."

Scottie smiled. This time it stayed. He felt as if he'd been given a gift. "Something like that, yeah." She unfolded her legs and pressed her palms against her thighs. "Stupid, huh?"

"No. Human."

"Yeah, well, I'm not accused of being that too often either," she said wryly.

"Then it's no wonder this is throwing you."

"What do you mean?"

"You paint yourself as this workaholic automaton who's suppressed her own feelings for the good of the company, completing mission after mission. Doesn't mean you don't have feelings and needs. You're just not used to being forced to deal with them."

She tilted her head. "Think you're pretty damn smart."

He grinned. "Know so."

"So why does someone so damn smart carry such a heavy burden of guilt around for something he had no control over?"

Logan felt as if he'd been sucker punched. "You're no slouch either. What did you major in, Insidious Interrogation Techniques one-oh-one?" He was grumbling, but he wasn't really upset. That surprised him enough to break eye contact. He dropped his chin, studied his hands.

"Minored," she shot back. "I majored in How to Turn the Tables to Keep from Answering Uncomfortable Questions."

Logan laughed as he looked up. "I bet you aced the course."

She beamed with mock pride. "Head of my class."

He shook his head. "We're a pair, aren't we?"

Scottie sobered a bit, but was still smiling. "We can successfully complete the most dangerous mission with dozens of lives at stake, but can't manage an interpersonal relationship past the rudimentary basics." She managed a dry laugh. "The perfect secret agents."

He looked at her. "Is that what you are?"

She looked right back at him. "Takes one to know one, doesn't it?"

Tellingly, he didn't answer. He leaned back on the couch, relaxing as he laughed. "We're hopeless. Hopeless."

Scottie nodded, smiling in agreement. Several moments passed, but the silence wasn't uncomfortable.

She watched Logan from the corner of her eye. He was lost in thought. She wished she knew what was rumbling around inside his head. She still wanted to know about Sarah, about Grant Hudson, about how he'd tracked down his brother when no one should have been able to find him. But even more, she wanted to know about things like his relationship with his father, what had made them open a bar together, what his life had been like growing up, who had he loved . . . which brought her right back to Sarah.

"You're right," he said, suddenly breaking the silence.

She looked at him. His expression had sobered and was once again unreadable. "About what?"

"Sarah."

"You didn't kill her."

He stared at her. "What exactly do you know about that?"

"Nothing. Only what I've heard from you. My background information on you is pretty slim, actually. Most of it's only as it pertains to your brother. We didn't have time to get much more. I didn't know about Sarah until I walked into that bedroom yesterday."

"Then how do you know I didn't kill her?"

"Instinct. You might blame yourself, but you didn't do it. Am I right?"

"You don't understand. She was in my protection."

"When you were working for the Detroit PD?"

"Yeah. She was a witness in a drug hit. Wrong place, wrong time. She had nothing to do with any of it. She agreed to testify, disagreed with protection of any kind." His focus turned inward, and for a moment a ghost of a smile crossed his lips. It was bittersweet and tugged at Scottie's heart. "She was a pretty self-reliant type," he said. "Didn't need anyone."

"What happened?"

"They killed her little brother." His expression turned to stone. "She agreed to protection then. She got her mother and her sister out of town. She stayed to testify. We were really shorthanded, and I ended up getting the baby-sitting assignment. It was my case and I was pretty upset, I could see the whole thing going down the toilet because she was too stubborn to stay safe."

"So you were more than happy to take the additional job."

"Sure was. We, uh, didn't get along real well, so I wasn't expecting to enjoy it. I just wanted her on that stand."

Scottie suppressed her smile. He was getting more uncomfortable by the moment, but not so much by the outcome of the story, which she could pretty well predict at this point. He was fidgeting because he was embarrassed.

"It's not a crime to fall in love, you know," she said, letting him off the hook.

He went stone still. "It is when you let your emotions cloud your judgment." When he looked at her this time, his eyes were so cold and empty, she shivered. "I got her killed as surely as if I'd held the gun to her head myself."

"She was a grown woman. She knew her life was in jeopardy. If she took a stupid risk and got herself nailed, you can't hold yourself responsible."

"The only stupid risk she took was falling in love with me. I knew my objectivity was shot, and I didn't call for a replacement. It was three days before she was scheduled to testify. We were in a safe house, and we got kind of, uh, involved. I got a call to move her. I thought she was safer with me." He looked her cold in the eyes. The emptiness she saw there chilled her. "She wasn't. By the time I realized how far wrong the situation had gone, she was dead and I was in intensive care." Hollow-eyed, he asked, "So you tell me. Who killed her?"

"You must have had a pretty good reason for not moving her." Scottie saw the argument coming and jumped defensively, not giving him a chance. "No, I don't buy the sex angle. You two could have been together whenever, wherever. There was another reason."

Logan looked away, then down at his hands. They were clenched in white-knuckled fists, the only outward clue to how deeply his emotions still ran.

"There was, wasn't there." It was a statement. His silence had answered the question.

After a moment, he said, "I was pretty sure I knew who the leak was, and I thought he was part of the team that I would have handed her over to. When he contacted me, that confirmed it. He wasn't the signal man. I knew it was a setup."

"So she was dead either way."

"No dammit!" he exploded. "I shouldn't have stayed where I was either. I should have gotten the hell out and gone on the run."

"Gone renegade? That's never a safe bet."

"That's what I thought. I didn't think he'd make a move on the safe house we were in. No time to set it up, and the team moving us didn't know where they were contacting, just who. I was wrong. He wasn't working alone. I was very careful, vetting everyone else out. I'd eliminated everyone but him. I never even suspected the other two. When I didn't move her, they contacted Renaldo's guys and it went down that night."

"You were lucky to survive."

The look he gave her made it clear he didn't share her assessment. "I woke up about two A.M. Something didn't feel right. I ran a thorough recon, but there was nothing. Still, I woke Sarah up. I wanted to move her right then. She, ah, didn't."

The light dawned. He didn't have to spell out the

rest. Scottie could pretty much figure it out. Sarah had persuaded him to stay in bed a few minutes longer, and it had proved a crucial mistake.

"We were moving out when they hit. I sent her ahead, thinking they were coming in from the front. I'd hoped to pull them off of her, let her get away. They got me. Tried to make me talk, tell them where she was. When force didn't work, they switched to chemical persuasion."

"Logan, no." His aversion to needles. "I'm so sorry."

He went on as if he hadn't heard her.

"I have no idea what I said after a while, but I didn't know where she'd run to, so I couldn't have told them much. I could only hope that she stayed wherever she'd gone to ground until someone figured out that things had gone wrong and came looking for one or both of us."

"She didn't stay safe," Scottie said.

Logan shook his head. "She came back. To save me. She never had a chance. I saw her cut down not fifty yards away from me."

"They didn't try to kill you, too, at that point?"

"Nope. Left me there to go through withdrawal. I was pretty bad off at that point. I'm sure they thought I'd be long dead by the time anyone found me. But I'd sure as hell suffer first."

"You'd think they'd be afraid if you somehow survived that you'd talk about the conspiracy, give up the dirty cops."

"I had no way of proving my theory. I saw no one I could identify. If I lived, I'd be the target of a massive investigation. Either way, their goal had been achieved."

"You didn't stay and fight it, did you?"

"I gave a statement, told them my suspicions. By the time I got out of the hospital, the preliminary investigation had been completed and I'd been cleared. But they had also failed to prove my allegations. The other three officers remained on the force. My father's health was beginning to decline. I took early retirement."

He hadn't spoken overdefensively, if anything he'd been quite the opposite, yet she knew he was waiting for her to argue about his decision. Apparently she would be one of many who had done the same thing.

"I'm not too sure, in your position, I'd have done differently. In any of it. You still blame yourself, don't you?"

"It was my fault she died, Scottie. There isn't any way around that. I shouldn't have become personally involved."

Scottie looked at him, her mind filled with visions of what that night had probably been like, the horrific outcome, and went still. Hadn't she been about to make that same mistake? Or was it already too late? Was she already personally involved? Was her judgment clouding?

"Do you really think you made the call not to move her based on your personal feelings? Wasn't that a judgment call based on your suspicions on the dirty cops? Suspicions backed by research that ultimately proved true?"

He shook his head. "It was never proven."

"But you still think you were right. To this day you know they were responsible."

"They're still on the force for all I know" was his only answer.

"And Renaldo?"

An unholy light flashed in Logan's eyes. For the first time she wondered exactly what this man was capable of.

"He got off that time. No testimony, no conviction."

"That time," she repeated.

"He was taken down about three years ago."

"By whom?" As soon as she asked, she knew the answer. "Grant Hudson," she whispered.

"It was a team effort," was all he said.

She didn't bother asking him to elaborate. He wouldn't. Anymore than she would or could about her own assignments or her affiliation with the Dirty Dozen. There was one other thing she wanted to know.

"Your team, Uncle Sam? Or private?"

He waited a beat, then said, "What do you think?"

"I think you wanted Renaldo dead and someone knew this and used it to recruit you. I think you received highly advanced training from this person or persons and, after successfully nailing Renaldo, decided to stay on. I think you enjoyed the freedom of having a bit more autonomy in enforcing the law. I think you enjoyed being part of a team that worked out of the limelight. I think you especially enjoy working alone."

"Pretty thorough assessment of someone you hardly know."

"Let's just say I recognize the character traits."

"Yeah, I got that part figured out already. You didn't answer my question."

"You mean, the question you answered my question

with? Uncle Sam," she said. "After what happened with Sarah and your department's inconclusive investigation, I think you liked the outlaw appeal of working behind the scenes. But ultimately, you still believe in justice the American way." She smiled. "You're not a total renegade. Yet."

He surprised her by smiling back. "Yet."

It was as close to a confirmation as she was likely to get.

"What made you go solo?" he asked.

She'd known this was coming. It was, after all, only fair to expect her to give a pint after she'd forced him to open a vein. She'd expected it to be more of a struggle, but in the end, she spoke easily.

"It was a pretty dramatic situation, but very different from yours."

"What force were you on?"

"Metropolitan D.C."

He made a face. "And I thought Detroit was a rough deal."

She shrugged. "It was my hometown PD, same as yours." Their shared understanding and common experience warmed her, settled her in a way she could never recall feeling. "My father and husband were also on the force." And she'd never felt any of this with either of them. Quite the opposite, in fact.

Logan raised an eyebrow. "I bet that was interesting. My dad retired right after I made sergeant." He smiled. "Didn't make things a damn bit easier, either."

"I understand that." More than he could ever know. "You and your dad were close, weren't you?"

"Despite all the bluster and constant nagging, you

mean? Yeah, we were close. We only ever had each other."

"Was he happy when you decided to become a cop?"

"Happy? No. Proud? Oh yeah. I'm surprised his badge didn't pop off, his chest was so swelled."

"But not happy?"

"He worried. It's not an easy life. But you know that."

Scottie looked down. "Yeah, I know that."

Lost in the midst of bitter memories, she didn't feel him shift his weight on the couch, didn't know he'd moved closer until she felt the touch of his hand beneath her chin.

"Your dad, he wasn't happy or proud, was he?"

She simply shook her head. How had she ever looked into his eyes and felt chilled? she wondered. She couldn't fathom it at the moment.

"And your husband? Did you marry before you were a cop?"

"After."

"And he disapproved?"

"You have to understand. His dad and my father were old cop buddies. They made it their life's work to toss us together at every opportune and inopportune moment. I'm not sure whose idea it finally was to get married, ours or theirs."

"Did you love each other?"

Her smile was wistful and more than a bit sad. "I'm not sure I remember. Maybe. Maybe we thought we did." She shrugged and pulled her chin from his grasp. "Maybe I just convinced myself I was in love to make my father happy."

"And did it?"

Her laugh was hollow. "For about the length of the wedding ceremony."

"What happened?"

"I didn't follow the plan. They all, my new husband included, thought that now that I was married, I'd quit the force, stay home, make grandbabies, and revel in my domestic bliss."

Logan's laugh was full and deep. "Oh man, major mistake."

Scottie just stared at him. "You know me better after a day and a half than they did during a lifetime."

"Maybe that's because I don't have a vested interest in seeing you as anything more or less than you really are."

She thought about that for a moment.

"And, for the record, I like who you really are. Well, except for your penchant for needles. That we have to talk about."

Scottie grinned and felt it reach way down deep. She didn't think she'd ever felt so truly complimented. "Thanks." She was afraid if she said anything more, she might get teary-eyed. As it was, her throat felt a bit tight. "I'll make a note on the needle thing."

"You do that." Logan's expression evened out a bit, though a light continued to warm his dark eyes. "So I guess things didn't go so smoothly when you told them you were staying on the force."

"Oh, you could say that. World War Three would have been easier to ride out."

"Your dad really hated you being a cop that much?"

"Oh, it wasn't just being a cop, something he was old-world enough to believe was a man's job. He felt it was my duty to marry and raise a nice, stable family. As I grew older, I understood more about why he was always so hard on me."

"Understanding doesn't always make it easy."

"Sounds like the voice of experience there." She realized he might be talking about what happened with Sarah as much as about his own relationship with his dad.

"Yeah, but although my dad was a hardheaded SOB on occasion, I never doubted he loved me or that he was proud of me. I don't know what I would have done in a situation like yours. I'm surprised you wanted to be a cop."

"I actually thought that once I did it, and he saw how good an officer I was, he'd be proud. I was wrong. My mom died of cancer when I was four. My dad never got over being mad at her for that. It wasn't right for a man to raise a daughter alone as far as he was concerned."

"Why didn't he remarry?"

"He might have been mad at my mother, but he was also religious. You only married once."

"Until death do you part."

"Well, he took that to mean both of them, I guess."

"Not knowing the real story, I always figured my dad was the same way. You know, you only have one love in a life. He never talked about my mother. He never remarried either. He sure bugged me about it, though."

Scottie nodded. "Exactly. He was so bent on me getting married and doing it 'the right way.' Then he could enjoy the family I created and be taken care of again."

"You didn't want children?"

She sighed. "It wasn't that. I didn't know what I wanted. I never really had the chance to think about it without all the added pressure. I did decide to be a cop because he was, but once I was in the academy, I knew I'd found something I truly loved doing. He never really understood that. Never. If anything, the fact that I was good at it made me even more of a failure to him. As a woman and as a person. Don't get me wrong, I have nothing against staying home to raise children. Who knows, had I met the right man, I might have given my father his dream without him ever asking for it. I'll never know. All I know is I found my niche, I found something that gave something back for what I put in." She looked at him and smiled ruefully. "I'd been on the force for five years when I got married. I made sergeant eighteen months later. I knew it wouldn't go over very well, so when I told them, I went ahead and dropped the whole bomb and told them I'd decided I wanted to go for detective."

Logan's eyes widened. "And you lived?"

Scottie smiled sadly. "Barely." She sobered, her voice quieting as she continued. "By then my marriage was worse than lousy, which is saying something since it was never all that great. Jim, my husband, more or less took up where my father left off. Nothing I did was right, I was a constant disappointment, whether it was my cooking, my housekeeping skills, even my police work."

"Why didn't you leave the bastard?"

She looked at him flatly. "Even though I hated how they treated me, and fought it constantly, I still deluded myself into believing that someday, if I just stuck it out long enough, they'd see that I was right and be proud of what I'd done. I know it sounds stupid, but when you're in the middle of it, that's all you have. I couldn't just walk away from my family. And if I filed for divorce, I wouldn't have had to worry about that. They'd have walked away from me." She paused for a moment. She felt his fingers push the hair back from her cheek and smooth along her ear. He rubbed the back of her neck.

Simple gestures, yet they almost undid her. No one, not once, not ever, had thought of her comfort, much less taken it upon themselves to soothe her.

When she continued, her voice was shaky and subdued. "I got my gold shield on Christmas Eve, eleven years ago. I had a huge fight with Jim, who called his father and mine over to yell at me some more. Like I was going to give it back when I'd worked so damn hard—" She broke off as her throat closed over.

Logan immediately tugged her closer, pulling her gently into his arms. She should have fought him, but it felt too damn good. He was offering a sanctuary she'd never known existed, and she wasn't strong enough to resist.

"I'm sorry," Logan whispered. He turned her so she was cradled in his lap, her legs stretched out along the couch. He pulled her head to his chest. "You don't have to—"

Eyes burning with emotion, she pulled back and looked at him. She had to finish. "In front of all three of them, I told him that I was filing for divorce and walked out. I ended up in a hotel. Twelve hours later my father and Jim were called out to a riot scene that broke out downtown Christmas morning."

Understanding dawned in Logan's eyes as he did the mental calculation. "The Christmas Massacre. I remember it. Your dad was—"

"Was one of the officers killed. Jim too. Jim's dad survived. So did I. By the time we were sent to the scene, the National Guard had been called out. I was never in danger. Jim's dad never forgave me. Said it was my fault, that my father and Jim were so upset that they couldn't have been thinking clearly."

"That's bull—"

Scottie pressed her fingers against his mouth. "I know that. Just like you know that Sarah dying wasn't your fault. Not really."

He pulled her hand away. "Not the same thing. It was my decision not to move her that directly caused the chain of events that killed her. You didn't start those riots."

"Logan—"

"Okay, okay, I'll shut up." He pressed his forehead against hers. After a moment of silence, he said, very quietly, "Maybe I'm starting to understand that no matter what I did that night, I might have lost her anyway. I don't think I'll ever excuse myself entirely, though. I can't. Some of the guilt is mine."

She carefully lifted her head and looked him in the eyes. "See, that's just it. I don't feel guilty because I thought it was my fault they died. I feel guilty because the moment it was confirmed to me that they had both died, I should have been overcome with grief and anguish."

"You felt those things, Scottie. It was a harrowing day. Six other police officers died along with a score of civilians. You can be excused for being in shock and not—"

"I wasn't in shock. And what I felt was relief. Stone-cold relief." She hung her head. "I'll never forgive myself for that."

TEN

Logan was all set to debate the issue, but bit off the argument at the last second. Who was he to preach to her about unwarranted guilt?

Unwarranted. He *was* actually beginning to think of what happened with Sarah a bit more objectively. He knew he would never entirely excuse himself and didn't feel he should. His decisions, good or bad, had played a role in her death. There was no way around that fact. But the condemning aspect of the guilt was receding, along with some of the anguish.

He looked at the woman he held in his arms. She was responsible. She made him think about things in an entirely different way. Maybe it was because she'd had a background similar to his, though he'd never once been tempted to date a fellow cop. No, it went much deeper than that. His connection to her was . . . instinctive, as if he knew her. *Knew* her. Sharing similar careers didn't create a bond like theirs. This connection was soul to soul.

Once the words sprang to his mind, he couldn't ignore the basic truth of them. Sarah had captured his heart and his imagination, but this woman had captured something far more valuable. She'd captured his spirit, his very soul. She had connected to the man he truly was, every layer, good and bad. She made him feel . . . accepted.

His throat grew tight, and his eyes were suddenly itchy. He tucked her head against his chest to buy a moment or two to get ahold of the emotions that had suddenly swamped him. But the moment she nestled her cheek to his chest, the battle only intensified.

"What did you do after they died?" he asked gruffly.

She snuggled closer. His heart squeezed another notch tighter.

He felt more than heard her gentle sigh. "I buried them. With all the media hoopla surrounding the aftermath of the riots, it was an exhausting time. After that, I stayed on the force. As a detective. Everyone was very sympathetic."

"You had a hard time dealing with that, didn't you?"

She lifted her head and stared at him, her expression a mix of wonder and gratitude. "Yes, I did. With everything going on, I was wiped out. I doubt anyone noticed that it was more exhaustion that made me pale and tired looking, rather than overwhelming grief."

"You grieved, Scottie. Maybe not the way you think you should have, but it still tore a hole in your life."

She thought about that for a moment, then said, "Maybe you're right. I grieved for what should have been. For the type of family I so badly wanted us to be, for the family we never could be now." Her eyes were a bit glassy as she continued to stare up at him. "You know, to this day, you are the only one who's ever truly understood all this. Understood the way I felt." She blinked hard several times. "Thank you. Thank you for making it okay."

"Maybe you should have given someone the chance to hear you out before this." Even as he said it, he knew she wouldn't have. He'd trusted her with a piece of himself, feelings he'd never shared before, because somehow he'd known she would understand. He sensed she had just done the same with him.

"No," she said, confirming his intuition. "I was ashamed of how I felt, but it didn't change the fact that I did feel the way I did. No one would have understood something like that. I was never big into discussing my personal problems with anyone."

Until now, he thought. And she'd chosen him to confide in. He'd have said she'd chosen unwisely except for one incontrovertible fact: He did understand.

"I'm sure it was no secret that we weren't a loving, close family, but—"

"On the surface you dealt with it," he finished for her. "In public and at work you probably even joked about it, deflected all sorts of questioning looks and comments with a well-chosen word or toss-away one-liner."

"You sure you worked Detroit and not my precinct?" She tried to make it a joke, but there was a slight wide-eyed look about her that made it fall just short of the mark.

He knew that feeling, he was experiencing the same one. "Spooky, isn't it?"

"Yeah, you could say that," she said softly. After a moment, she glanced away almost shyly. It was a sweet surprise, another side to Scottie he'd bet his bottom dollar not many, if any, suspected existed.

"Why not transfer to another force?"

"I thought about it. Start over, create a whole new life. I had an application into San Francisco. I did my research. I thought I had a good shot there."

"What happened?"

"I got another job offer. A better one."

"Working for Uncle Sam?"

She nodded. "You know, it's been eleven years since they died. This should be easier to talk about."

"But you haven't ever talked about it, have you? Time doesn't heal all wounds, especially the ones that are never dealt with. They are left to fester."

She nodded against his chest, then smiled up at him. "I think this one is on its way to healing now. Thanks, Doc."

"Just returning the favor, Doc." Logan cuddled her closer, reveling in the way she immediately curled against him. Acceptance. The word floated through his mind again.

It was a heady thing to think she felt as accepted by him, flaws and all, as he did by her. Amazing even to think in terms of acceptance. If anyone had ever asked him, he'd have quite honestly told them he didn't give a rat's behind what anyone thought of him. He'd have never guessed just how badly he needed to be truly understood and accepted this way. Powerful, earthshaking stuff.

He pressed his lips to her hair, kissing her softly as he drank in the scent of her. He felt drunk on the rainbow of sensations and emotions cascading through him. He didn't want to be sober ever again.

"You never told me the whole story," he said.

"What story?"

"Anunsciata."

"Oh. That story." When he didn't say anything right away, he felt her laugh softly into his shirt. "Go ahead, do your worst," she said. "I'm immune."

"No jokes." But a moment later he said, "Your father really did have it in for you from day one, didn't he?"

She laughed louder this time, the deep timbre vibrating against his skin . . . and his heart.

"My mother's grandmother's middle name was Anunsciata. Old-world Italians, very religious."

"I'm almost afraid to ask what your middle name is."

Scottie looked up and smiled. "Bernadina. After my father's favorite great-aunt."

Logan made a face. "Poor kid."

"Yeah, well, Scottie was better than Bernie, to me anyway. I tried to focus on that."

He grinned. "Boy, I bet you hated getting in trouble." When she looked confused, he said, "Didn't your dad pull the full name out when you broke the rules? I think I would have done just about anything to not hear 'Anunsciata Bernadina!' "

She laughed, nodding. "Yeah, he was the type. It made for some embarrassing moments in roll call."

Logan's eyes widened. "Roll call?"

"You don't think he stopped just because I grew up? It got worse as I got older." Her eyes sparkled. "Especially when I outranked him."

"Another lifetime beat cop? Man, your dad and mine together could have been scary. My dad lived by the creed that it was the patrolmen against the chain of command. He routinely threatened to retire every time they tried to promote him. Eventually they gave up." He smiled fondly. "He was one hell of a beat cop, though. Made it his business to know everybody in his neighborhood and made damn sure they all knew him."

"Sounds like a man to admire. Wish I'd had the pleasure of meeting him."

"Me too," Logan said. "Even after he retired, which he only did when his body finally stopped passing the annual physicals, and opened up Blackie's, he still kept current with everything that was going on. The bar was a hangout for cops and locals alike. Everyone was comfortable at Blackie's place. He used to say it was his contribution to community relations to make sure cops and citizens got drunk together every once in a while."

"I bet he's terribly missed," she said.

"It was a helluva wake, aye, it was." Logan thought back on the three-block-long street party that had lasted on through the night and well into the dawn hours. "Yeah, he's missed," he said quietly.

"I'm sorry, Logan," she said just as softly.

He looked down at her. "Me too. He was all I had."

"Until now."

For a moment, Logan froze. His immediate thought was that she was referring to herself. It was what he'd thought of when she'd said it. But she meant—

"I can't imagine how it must feel. A brother, a twin no less," she said. "It's so amazing. I know it was a shock, but it's also a blessing. Other than the fact that I'd never have wanted to subject anyone else to my father's tyranny, I've always wondered what it would have been like to have a brother or sister. You were an only child. Didn't you ever wish for siblings?"

"Maybe. I guess so. Probably not the way you did. I spent a few years around puberty wishing I had a mother, but my dad and I were close. Our place was always full of other cops and their wives and kids. I was never lonely. Then I discovered girls and well . . ." He wiggled his eyebrows, wanting to make her laugh.

Strangely, he didn't want to talk about Lucas with her. Not because he didn't want to know more about him. She probably knew more about his mysterious twin than anyone else. He did want to pick her brain, find out all he could. Just not right at that moment.

Right now, he didn't want to share her with anyone, not with his phantom brother, not even with memories of their pasts. Right at this moment, he wanted her all to himself, wanted her attention focused exclusively on the here and now. He wanted *her*.

She did laugh. "I can see where girls could dominate a young boy's thoughts."

"What about you?" he asked, smiling despite the increasing desire clawing at his insides.

"Think about girls?" she tossed back with mock sincerity. "Nah. I mean, I was sort of butch, but—"

Logan's laughter rang full and deep. It felt wonderful. He hugged her. "In your case I was talking about boys. Didn't you fall in and out of love on a regular basis when you were twelve or thirteen?"

"Nope. I've been a one-man woman from the start." She sighed dramatically and patted her heart. "Matt Liganotti. We fell in love in science class. We shared the same frog. You should have seen his dissecting skills." She fluttered her eyelashes. "Thick glasses and red hair. What a babe." She giggled. "I'd forgotten all about him."

The innocent sound, coming from someone whose childhood sounded as if it had been anything but, charmed him. He loved that he could give pieces of the good times back to her.

"He probably never got over you."

"Oh, I never actually let him know. Heaven forbid." She rolled her eyes. "My father was rather clear from the time I was like, seven, that there would be no dating until I was at least twenty, and then only with a chaperon, meaning him." She shuddered. "Can you imagine? That was the downside of being a cop's daughter. Every boy, no matter his background, was a potential drug dealer or rapist."

He knew she was exaggerating, but probably not as much as she should have been. "It wasn't much easier being the son of a cop," he said. "God help my hide if I ever got caught necking in my car."

She grinned. "Did you?"

"Necking?" He cleared his throat. "Uh, no."

She laughed out loud and smacked his chest. "You didn't?"

He nodded, trying to cover a grin with a sober, penitent look. She clearly didn't buy it for a second. "Mary Louise Redenbacher."

She eyed him with a disapproving frown. "Well, I only have one thing to say about that."

"Which is?" he asked warily.

She beamed a devilish grin of her own. "Was she worth it?"

He choked on a surprise laugh but quickly recovered. "Oh yeah." He added a heartfelt sigh. "Both times."

She thumped his chest again in mock effrontery, and

he laughed. She tried not to join him, but he kept it up until she collapsed against him, giggling until she was gasping for air.

He tipped her chin up until she looked at him. Her eyes were alive with delight, her wide smile invited him to smile along with her. Simply put, she knocked his socks off.

Kissing her seemed like the most natural thing in the world to do. Her eyelids slid half closed as his mouth neared hers, her smile changed to parted lips that invited something else entirely. It was an invitation he couldn't have refused even if it had meant imminent death.

"You're one of a kind, Scottie Giardi," he whispered.

A slight smile curved her lips. "Better than Mary Louise Redenbacher?"

"Why don't we find out?"

She was laughing as he took her mouth. It quickly changed to a deep-throated moan.

"I want you, Scottie. I don't think I've ever wanted anyone this way."

She pushed back enough to look in his eyes. Sarah, again, he thought, somewhat disappointed. He didn't want her to dwell on the past any longer. For the first time in what felt like forever, he was looking forward to the future. Hoping he wasn't letting his irritation show, he said, "Listen—"

She spoke at the same time. "Yeah, but how are you at dissecting frogs?"

It took a second for the question to register. Delight filled him. "Have no idea," he said. "I let Marcia Johnson slice mine open. She wielded a pretty mean scalpel."

"I'll just bet she did."

He buried his face in her neck. "There's only one thing I want to examine up close and personal." He nibbled along the edge of her jaw.

"Oh?" The word was more like a soft gasp.

He loved watching her sharp eyes grow a little misty and unfocused. "Yes, oh." He drew his tongue along her lower lip, then pulled it gently with his teeth. "Mmmm . . . mine," he said, then covered the rest of her mouth with his.

Scottie sank willingly as waves of sensations rolled over and through her. It wasn't just physical desire that held her in thrall. Oddly, that was almost a side benefit. In his arms, she had an inescapable sense of homecoming. With Logan she felt an inner relaxation, a loosening up of an integral part of her that she'd held in steely check for as long as she could remember. Logan understood her.

Somehow, she'd known he would. Was that why she'd decided to open up and tell him about a past she hadn't discussed with anyone in ten years? Because he made her feel safe? She almost laughed at the idea. The very last thing she felt around Logan Blackstone was safe.

And yet, she was.

His lips drew a soft, warm line down her throat, nuzzling aside her turtleneck to explore even farther. She felt a sudden, desperate need to rip every scrap of clothing from her body . . . and from his. She wanted to drown in the exquisite sensations that would surely saturate her every pore if she could only feel his skin against hers.

"Logan, I need—" She broke off on a gasp as he found her ear.

"Need, yes," he rumbled.

"Clothes," she managed.

"No clothes," he said, breathing as heavily as she.

"No. I mean yes." She gasped as he levered off her enough to yank both his shirts off with one violent tug. "Yes, definitely no clothes."

She clawed at her own shirt, scrambling to peel the long, snug sleeves from her arms, her eyes riveted to the broad expanse of chest hovering above her, wanting with a need akin to desperation, to feel that tightly wrapped skin pressed against her own. She thought she would explode from frustration when she couldn't get the thing off over her head.

"Let me." With a tug it was gone and he was back, his chest filling her entire range of vision. He was already working on her pants, shimmying them down her hips. Somewhere along the line, probably when she was wrestling with her shirt, his pants had managed to disappear. Then he was on top of her and they were both blissfully naked. It was even more incredibly wonderful than she'd imagined. She wanted to take time, hours to explore his body, enjoying every inch of her travels, but other needs dominated.

She sunk her fingers into all that dark, thick hair and pulled his face down to hers. Later. She'd investigate to her heart's content later. "Now," she demanded. His grin was past wicked even as he raised a questioning brow. "Logan," she warned.

"Your command is my wish," he said, making her smile even as the ache between her legs threatened to paralyze her. He nudged her legs apart. Broad hands pulled her thighs up over his hips as he angled himself above her.

Her breath caught in her throat. He was nothing short of magnificent and, for right now, he was all hers. He slowly slid inside her, filling her so perfectly, so completely. This went deeper than satisfaction, this meant more than simply finding release. At that crystalline moment, her life was perfectly balanced, her soul was in complete harmony. She struggled to grasp the meaning of it all, but then he began to move deep inside her and all thoughts of inner peace and homecoming slid into the netherworld of her mind as more primal directives took over.

"Hold me tight." He cupped her hips and rolled them both onto their sides, pressing her back into the couch, her leg high on his hip.

She was surrounded by him, yet she surrounded him as well, gripping him oh so tightly.

"Open your eyes, Scottie. Look at me," he commanded.

She did. His face was carved into a harsh relief of sharp angles and smooth planes, his expression was fierce, his eyes flashing blacker than midnight, wild and primeval. She felt no fear. Her ferocity of need, her depth of emotion matched what she found there.

"There's no one else here, nothing between us, do you understand that?" he said roughly.

She nodded.

"This is—" He broke off on a groan as she shifted, still holding him tightly, deep within her. His voice hardly more than a raspy whisper. She felt him tighten up, as if exercising incredible restraint.

"This is what, Logan?" She knew what it was rapidly becoming to her and held her shallow breath in check.

"This is . . . a defining moment." He pulled her closer, shifted a bit, slid more deeply inside her. She sensed his control unraveling. "Do you understand?" He held her gaze in total lockdown. She couldn't speak, couldn't even nod. "Dear God, I'm not even sure I do," he managed. "All I know is that I want you—us—to remember this exact moment. Always."

He gave her no time to respond. A loud growl erupted from deep in his throat as his control broke. His head reared back as he gripped her hips tightly to his and buried himself fully inside her. The guttural half-groan, half-moan continued as he moved into her again and again.

"Come with me." It was a hoarse plea. It was all she needed.

As if a rip cord had been yanked deep inside her, with one final thrust she was whipped up and over the edge, convulsing around him as he rocked and shuddered.

He rolled to his back and would have fallen off the couch if she hadn't reached out and pulled him back against her.

He pressed his cheek to her temple. "I'll crush you."

"I'm made of pretty strong stuff," she whispered. When he tried to move again, she tightened her hold. "Don't, not yet."

He didn't pause, didn't question, he pulled her more tightly to him, then shifted until she was sprawled on top of him.

He smiled up at her surprised expression. "Compromise."

Now it was her turn to try and lift her weight off him. "I'm no lightweight."

She thudded back down against him, steel bands masquerading as arms strapping her down.

He grinned at her and kissed her nose. "You're perfect. Put your head right here." He gently pressed her cheek to his chest. "Let me do this." His fingers began an almost hypnotic, slow massage through her hair.

"I feel like purring," she murmured, languor creeping into her muscles, melting them one at a time under his touch.

"You like to be stroked," he said approvingly.

"Actually, no." She wanted to lift her head, look at him, but her head felt like a lead weight. His fingertips raked against her scalp, and she gave up without trying. She settled more heavily against him. He didn't seem to mind. He sighed and let his fingers trail down her back. She had to work to remember her train of thought. Stroking. "I—I've always been irritated by light touches. Always wanted to smack it away, like an annoying fly. I—ah, oh does that feel good." She groaned in pleasure. "Are those hands licensed?"

"Not for this."

Her smiling moan hummed against the steady beat of his heart. "They should be registered weapons. Lethal."

"I'm glad you enjoy my touch," he said intently. "I enjoy stroking you very much. I could spend hours doing this."

"I'm not going anywhere."

He chuckled. "Good."

"I promise I'll return the favor." She sighed deeply

as he trailed his fingers along her neck and down her arms. "Someday."

"I just might hold you to that."

"Hold me, yes." She sighed. She fell silent, allowing herself to sink into his touch. Her thoughts drifted, lazed about in no real coherent pattern. Pure escape. "Decadent," she murmured. "I've never felt so decadent and pampered."

"You haven't been living right."

"I haven't been living," she said, half dazed with pleasure. "I know I should feel guilty for enjoying this," she murmured against his chest, "but it feels too damn good to be responsible."

He tilted his chin down, and she felt the gentle pressure of his lips on her hair. "You're much too hard on yourself," he said softly. "If it will make you feel better, consider this your belated Christmas present."

The lassitude ebbed. Christmas. She looked up, scraping her hair from her face, not realizing she was searching for the reassurance of his eyes, his smile, until she locked onto it.

"I guess Christmas doesn't hold real fond memories for you, does it?" He lifted a hand and carefully stroked away the hair that still clung to her cheeks.

"Never has. Growing up it was a time of tension. For the last ten years it's just been an anniversary to get through."

"I'm sorry."

"It's okay. Really. I'm used to it."

"No, I'm sorry I reminded you of it. I find that I very much enjoy bringing you pleasure. You gave me a gift, letting me stroke you, enjoying my touch. Only my touch. Amazing how good that makes me feel." He pressed a kiss to his finger and brushed it across her lips. "I'm also finding that I hate being responsible for you suffering any kind of pain."

She stared into his eyes as his sincere words penetrated the final wall around her heart. All the tension drained out of her. "I've never met a man like you, Logan Blackstone."

"Just one that looks exactly like me," he teased.

She returned his grin. "How do you do that?"

He looped his arms comfortably across her back. "Which wonderful thing would you be referring to?"

"You say the most amazing things to me, you make my throat all tight and achy, then you make me smile and laugh and—" She broke off knowing she couldn't begin to explain what he made her feel. Instead she kissed him hard on the lips. "Thank you."

"You're welcome. And please, thank me again anytime."

She smiled, but her eyes were glassy. "Really, you've made me—You've made this—I can't explain how you—"

He silenced her with a heartbreakingly sweet kiss.

She would seize this perfect moment in time. Nothing had been jeopardized by what she'd done, nor would it be. She could carve out this little niche of happiness for herself and enjoy it without hurting anyone. She could and she would. For right now. She would doubt her actions and worry over possible repercussions later.

"Would you like to make it a Merry Christmas again?" she asked, her slow smile fueled by her decision. She didn't see the point in wasting what little time she would have.

Logan apparently understood this too. He grinned

and leaned to whisper in her ear. "Does Santa Claus wear red?" Just as he kissed her earlobe, a warm hum vibrated the soft skin. Logan shifted his head, a questioning smile on his face. "I'd like to think it's my electric personality, but if I'm not mistaken, your earring is buzzing."

Del. Her once-in-a-lifetime interlude evaporated like an ephemeral mist.

ELEVEN

It wasn't until Logan asked, "Who's Del?" that Scottie realized she'd spoken out loud. She was already climbing off of him. A strong hand stopped her in midscramble.

"Who is Del?"

She looked at him. The implacable mask was back on his face. "He was—is—my boss. I have to contact him." She looked at his hand on her arm, then back at him. "Now."

"Interesting pager you wear."

"Yeah well, the standard-issue beeper just doesn't work in all cases. But I suspect you're familiar with spy toys."

"Can't say as I've ever worn an earring pager, but it could happen. Yes."

Scottie smiled a bit distractedly, worrying about what Del had to report. There was still so much about Logan she hadn't had time to find out, so many questions she wanted to ask him. A lifetime of questions. She shut down that train of thought with a firm slap. "I'm sure you also understand how important it is to respond to incoming calls in a situation like this."

As soon as she'd said the words, she wished she could have taken them back. Sarah. She knew from the sudden steel in his eyes he thought she was making a not-so-veiled comment about his episode with Sarah.

"Logan, I didn't mean it like—"

"No, I understand," he cut her off. He sounded hard, distant, not at all the man she had just made love with. The man she was falling in love with. No, she commanded herself. Don't even go there.

"You're right," he said. "Playtime is over. Guess I should go back to being a captive 'under your protection' like a good little boy, huh?"

Scottie's heart felt as if a nail had been driven into it. It's not like that, she wanted to yell at him. But wasn't it exactly like that? She'd known this little interlude was temporary and that it would end too soon, but she hadn't expected it to be jerked out from under her. She didn't want to focus on the crushing sense of loss she was feeling. He was right too. Her job had to come first. Maybe it was just as well it had ended before she fell the rest of the way in love with him. Dammit. "You don't need to do anything except let me go."

"Then you're saying that when you're done contacting your boss, we can resume our . . . celebration?" His expression made it clear he expected no such thing.

Scottie let out a sigh and relaxed against his hold, which he then immediately dropped. "I can't promise you anything right at the moment," she said wearily. "We both know why I'm here. I'd think you'd be as interested in whatever Del has to report as I am. It's your brother out there."

"I am very interested in Del, my brother, and everything that is happening in that compound. I am also interested in making sure you don't run back to the safe shelter of your career."

Stung, she said, "Who's running? I have work to do, and all I'm asking is that you let me do it."

"And then what?"

"And then what *what*?"

"After you talk to Del and save the planet, then what?" He took her face in his hands. "Let me make it even clearer for you. You aren't just a roll on the couch, okay? I want more. Do you? Or are we done now that the job beckons?"

Scottie stilled, stunned by his admission. "More?"

"Much more."

She'd been so intent on capturing even a small scrap of time with him, she hadn't really thought of what came after. She hadn't allowed herself to. It hadn't occurred to her that he might want more too. The very idea dazzled her with possibilities. "I—" Her earlobe was buzzing almost continuously now. Not a good sign. "I really have to contact Del," she said. "Can we talk about this when I get done?"

He studied her for a moment.

"I *want* to discuss this, Logan. I want . . . more too. But Del wouldn't be buzzing me if it weren't important."

"Go." He released her instantly, his expression unreadable. He helped her off of him, and stood along with her, his touch impersonal despite their nakedness. She should have wanted to snatch her clothes and yank them on, but despite the current tension between them, she felt at ease with him, as if they'd argued and loved for so many years, their state of dress was irrelevant.

Then she turned and caught him staring at her, the dark hunger open and there for her to see . . . and understand. And she did understand it now. Thoroughly. Intimately.

The tension intensified, layered.

"Go make your call." Logan turned away, bent down to snag his jeans, and crossed to the bedroom. The door closed with a quiet snick.

Scottie's first inclination was to go pound on the door, demand they discuss this now and to hell with Del. There was a very real fear that if she didn't, that door would remain closed to her, at least figuratively, forever. Her earring buzzed like an angry bee. "Oh, shut up."

She cast one more glance at the bedroom, then swore under her breath. She'd been foolish to think it was her turn to have something—someone—all for herself. Throat tight, her heart feeling as if it were slowly being chiseled in two, she turned away and went in search of her digital phone.

Del answered immediately. He didn't bother with the code. "What in the hell is going on up there?"

His uncustomary gruffness reminded her of her father, and of Jim. She squared her shoulders and her jaw. She'd taken enough of a beating for one lifetime. No more. "Merry Christmas to you too. What's up?"

There was a telling pause, but when he spoke again, his tone had regained its customary implacable control. "We've lost Blackstone."

Scottie's gaze flew to the closed bedroom door. *"What?"*

"Still no contact. He's missed every check-in."

Then he wasn't dead. Not for certain anyway. The knot that had risen from her heart to her throat abided. "Don't scare me like that, dammit! Things are getting close. He might not have been able to make the calls."

"If we don't hear from him within twelve hours, we're going to go in."

"No." Scottie reached for her clothes, shifting the phone as she quickly pulled them on. "We act before Lucas has it set, and anything could happen. Those kids would be the first to go."

"If Lucas has been found out, then those children are dead anyway. Twelve hours is already pushing it."

Scottie knew what the contingency plan was, she'd designed it. They couldn't have had time to set it up. "His last report gave us no indication that he was in danger of discovery," Scottie responded. "Unless you know something I don't know." She chafed at being forced to ask for information that should have been for her eyes first.

"No, you saw the only report. However—"

"Then I say we hold out for twenty-four hours. Give him a chance. We don't know for certain he's been found out. The Brethren's rationale for timing this on New Year's Eve isn't coincidental. I don't think they will radically change those plans unless Blackstone tells them something. You and I both know he won't."

Scottie listened to the silence on the other end of the line. Tension vied with frustration. She shouldn't be questioning his judgment. Del was her mentor, had mounted and successfully completed hundreds of missions, but, dammit, this one was hers. Or had been.

She resisted the urge to fill the growing silence with continued arguments. Instead she took a different tack. "It's not like you to push so soon, Del. Where is the pressure coming from?"

"*Dios*, where isn't it coming from," he muttered.

"You're the champion in deflecting pressure from all sides. I can't believe they, whoever 'they' are, are getting to you." No response. "Is it that bad?"

A heavy sigh came over the line.

Scottie's frustration immediately fled. Never had she heard such a defeated sound from her former leader. "Seve?"

"I owe you an apology, Scottie. I don't even have time for a half decent attempt."

Alarmed now, Scottie broke in. "Listen, Del—"

"No, you listen!" He stopped long enough to moderate his tone. He spoke rapidly and precisely. "There are things happening here you know nothing about. It's better for the future of the team that you don't. That's the only reason I'm involved in this one. Maybe that was a mistake, and, if so, I'll take responsibility for it. But for now, you have to trust that I know what I'm doing. Blackstone has been compromised."

"Caught maybe, but never compromised." Scottie's mind was whirling in a dozen different directions, but not even Del's odd behavior could distract her from defending her team. "No way. You don't have proof of that."

"Blackstone's gotten . . . close to Martina Gladiston."

"The senator's daughter?"

"Apparently he's set her up to help him."

"He *what?* He told her who he really is?"

"Apparently she's not there as some defiant act against her father like we thought. She's there under-cover, doing a story on cults and paramilitary groups, and stumbled across the suicide plans."

"And Lucas, it appears. I didn't know she was a jour-nalist."

"She's not. Not yet anyway. She's hoping to use this story as her calling card. According to Lucas, she's had a hard time breaking into the industry due to her father's celebrity—"

"Notoriety, you mean," Scottie said sharply. She paced the length of the couch, then stalked to the kitchen counter. Senator Gladiston had made more headlines with his extracurricular activities than with his congressional ones. But the dashing politician managed time after time to land on his feet. Gladiston disgusted her, and she didn't hide her derision. "Regardless of Martina's reasons for being there—and frankly, being a journalist, to me, makes this worse—I have a really hard time believing he'd take that sort of risk with other lives on the line."

She turned to lean on the counter and found herself facing Logan, who was lounging in the now-open door-way to the bedroom. His raised eyebrow all but tossed her words back in her face. She wanted to tell him this was different. But was it? Heat crept up her neck, but she refused to turn or look away.

"I wasn't happy either," Del went on, "but he was dead set on this as the best course. You know I give my agents a great deal of latitude in fulfilling their assign-ments."

The heat rose like a flame to her cheeks as she watched Logan while Del's words branded her ear. Latitude. She had certainly, um, exercised that right. She cleared her throat and forced herself to forge ahead. "Yes, sir, I agree with you. I've long believed that our individual approach to each assignment is what makes us so successful."

There was a brief pause, and Scottie's heart paused along with it. Del couldn't suspect . . . could he? She found her gaze locked with Logan's. She hadn't compromised anything, she reminded herself. Liar, her heart responded. If something happened to Logan, could she absolutely promise her responding actions would be based on what was best for the success of the current mission? Or what was best for her personally?

"He knew I couldn't pull him out of there, not with the recent changes in plans." Del's gruff voice yanked her thoughts back to the matter at hand. "I ordered him to contain the situation as best he could without involving Ms. Gladiston." There was another short sigh, followed by a string of swear words, most of them Spanish.

If she hadn't been so worried and confused, she might have smiled. This sounded like the Del she'd worked for.

"I guess I should be getting used to losing that battle by now," he said. "Hearts are dropping like flies out there."

The team had taken many hits over the decade they'd been in existence, but none so crucial as the most recent changes. In fact, it had been those potential losses that had caused Scottie to take the team in a new direction. She had been given the job of not only running the team, but rebuilding it from the ground up.

With several agents losing their field credibility, she'd begun an interior team as well as an exterior, or field team.

"As much as you'd like us to be otherwise," Scottie said, "we are human."

This time the brief pause made her swallow. She'd said too much. "Sounds like you know whereof you speak," he said.

Wisely, she evaded a direct answer. He'd get his explanation when she got hers. Maybe by then she'd have an explanation to give him. "I know the team was close to being wiped out and that under my management and new direction, we'll thrive."

Del knew better than anyone how fragile an agent's necessarily inviolable status could be. His own past confirmed it. And if that weren't enough, one of the three agents they'd lost in the last three months, Diego Santerra, had lost his status by falling in love with Del's daughter, Blue, during an assignment.

Then there had been John McShane. He'd abandoned an assignment midstream to fly halfway around the world because a woman he hadn't seen in ten years had sent him a note saying she was in trouble.

The third agent had retired just weeks ago. Scottie vividly recalled the conversation she'd had with T. J. Delahaye in her office only weeks before. He'd been crawling out of his skin, trying to track down a woman he'd known for less than twenty-four hours. He'd been convinced this woman was his future.

Scottie had questioned him then, unable to fathom such a thing. But now . . .

Her attention was drawn unerringly to the man leaning negligently in the door frame, arms folded casually across a bare expanse of chest. A chest she'd been cradled against less than an hour before. A chest she wanted to be cradled against again. And again. Logan Blackstone.

A man she'd known less than a week.

How would she feel if Logan suddenly disappeared? Would she track him down as T.J. had done with Jenna? Would she be willing to give up her career as McShane and Santerra had been willing to do? If Logan really wanted more, as he'd said he did . . . well, what exactly did more mean? She knew from his experience with Sarah that when he committed, he committed fully. Every muscle she had tightened in anticipated pleasure at the thought of having Logan Blackstone committing himself to her. The idea overwhelmed her. The possibility thrilled her.

How much more did *she* want?

All, came the instant, resounding answer. She wanted it all.

"Maybe we only come with a ten-year guarantee," she told Del, suddenly fighting a smile. A powerful rush pounded its way through her veins. *Could* she really pursue this, whatever it was, with Logan? Should she? Again, the word yes reverberated inside her head. And her heart.

Del grunted at her suggestion. "Whatever the hell it is, it's making me old before my time."

"You're ageless," she said. And single. Hmm. Ideas and thoughts that she had no business thinking, crossed her mind. If Del so much as suspected them, he'd not only fire her, he'd have her committed. If someone had told her even a month earlier that she'd be having these thoughts, she'd have had herself committed. For some reason, that thought made her smile as well.

Logan began to walk across the room toward her. Her pulse thrummed, and her heart started a staccato beat. Could this man really be mine? she wondered. Forever?

"Ageless?" Del grunted. "I guess that's probably the one side benefit to having your appearance overhauled on a regular basis."

Her attention snapped back to the conversation. "Is that what you've done?" It made sense. If he changed often enough, he could run the team without compromising himself or them to the many enemies he'd racked up over the years, enemies who knew his real face from the drug trial. They could track him through a change or two, maybe, but after a while . . . "How many times?"

"Often enough."

"Then you are back."

"There is really no time for this, Giardi. Later. I promise you. Right now I've got an agent not reporting in, and a wanna-be journalist in way over her head, running wild in the compound doing God knows what. Without someone on the inside, Martina Gladiston is like a loose cannon. We have no idea what she might have done. I trust your skills as commander or I wouldn't have recommended you for the position, but I am pulling rank this time. I can't give you those twenty-four hours. We need to move now before—"

An idea popped into her head as Logan came to a stop directly in front of her. "What if I could give you an insider?"

"What?" Del sounded wary, but he was listening.

"I said, what if I could give you another inside agent. One who happens to look exactly like the agent already in there?"

After a moment, followed by another grudging sigh, Del responded. "I'd say it sounds as if this will definitely be your last field assignment."

He knew. Scottie should have felt chastened by his retort. Instead, she grinned at Logan as she said, "Yeah, that might be a safe bet."

"I should read you the riot act, Scottie, but I find I can't. Maybe I am getting too old for this."

"Seve—"

"Later. All of this will be handled later. For now, I want to talk to you about putting Logan inside the compound."

"He's highly trained, Del. He's—"

"I know what he is. I have the report right here in my hands. Your instincts are good, Giardi. I'm of the mind to agree with your proposal, except with his brother in there in heaven knows what circumstance, he could be a worse loose cannon than the senator's daughter."

Scottie wanted to drill Del on the contents of the file. She was dying of curiosity. But she'd have the time to read the file later. She caught Logan's steady gaze. Staring at him while she spoke, she said, "You can trust him, Del."

"His service record is a cause for concern. Some of the stunts he's pulled make our guys look like choirboys. The guy thinks he's the Lone Ranger or something."

She grinned at that. "James Bond," she corrected, "as played by Mel Gibson." Logan's mouth quirked into a sardonic smile, but he remained silent. Her smile faded under Logan's continued regard. He had to know enough from her end of the conversation what the gist of the situation was. He'd made no indication one way or another about his willingness to be involved, but Scottie knew. She looked into his black eyes and knew. She took his hand in hers, wove her fingers through his, and held on tight. He held on just as tightly and gave her a short nod.

"I'd trust him with my life, Del," she said quietly.

The pause this time was almost nonexistent. "Then let's do it. I'll hammer out the details with you and send in whatever you need. You get back to the location where you stowed the snowmobile. I can get a helivac unit in there without alerting too much attention. You'll be responsible for prepping Blackstone. It will be your show after that, Commander."

Scottie straightened her shoulders. Even knowing she'd compromised her field status by becoming personally involved with Logan, Del still trusted her. Her throat a bit tight, she said, "Yes, sir. I won't let you or the team down, sir."

"Of course you won't." Typical of Del, he didn't give her time for any further expression of gratitude. "Let's get down to business."

Logan listened to Scottie's end of the conversation and waited as patiently as possible for her to conclude and disconnect before speaking.

She turned to him, her face flushed, her eyes bright with anticipation. The wheels were turning at warp speed.

"You miss fieldwork, don't you?" He had a million questions, but for some reason this was the first thing on his mind.

It obviously surprised her as well. "I enjoy what I do for the team now. It's even more challenging than field-work."

"But it's still management. You like this playing on the edge, surviving on your wits."

"I'll admit I miss it. Sometimes. But I wouldn't go back." Her eyes widened slightly after she said it, as if she hadn't known it herself until then. "Not that it makes any difference at this point. My field status is shot."

Logan's expression hardened. "Why? You haven't done anything to compromise this mission. I'll talk to Del directly if you—"

Scottie stopped him with two fingers on his lips. "No, you won't." She smiled. "But thank you for wanting to defend me. It's a unique experience for me, but I find I'm liking it. You're more a white knight than you think you are."

"Hardly."

She pushed her fingers into his hair. "Okay, a dark knight then. Does that appeal more to your rogue warrior sensibilities?"

Logan actually felt his cheeks heat up. She was quite sincere. The combination of having earned Scottie's respect along with the feel of those fingers stroking his scalp was potent. "You don't know me, Scottie."

"Yes, I do." She looked intently into his eyes. "I am you."

He studied her long and hard, hearing the truth in her words, knowing them to be the truth deep inside his soul. If there was ever a woman who was his match, it was Scottie Giardi.

"I think maybe you are," he said gruffly. He pulled

her close to him. "Put your other hand on me, Scottie. I find I like to be stroked by you almost as much as I enjoy stroking you."

She came willingly, her other hand circling his neck, teasing the sensitive skin at his nape.

"You're a dangerous woman, Anunsciata Bernadina."

She grinned. "I do like hearing my name on your lips." She stepped in a little closer. "Now are you going to hurry up and kiss me before we are forced to get down to business, or am I going to have to play rough?"

"See, I knew there was more to this bondage thing with you." Logan grinned and pulled her hips tight. Her soft gasp sent his pulse pounding. "You're one breath away from finding yourself back on that couch."

"I wish," she said, her tone so heartfelt, he laughed even as he groaned.

"You'll be the death of me, Scottie."

She sobered immediately. "No. No, I won't." She took his face in her hands and kissed him hard on the mouth. When he tried to take it deeper, she pulled away. Even that short contact left them both breathing abnormally hard. "Promise me you will take every precaution inside that compound. You have to come back out of there in one piece, do you hear me?"

Logan felt his heart slip away. He let it go willingly, knowing she would keep it safe. "I hear you," he said softly. "You're right, you know."

"Of course I am." She smiled, the worry in her eyes abating slightly. "About what?"

"About it being a pretty nice thing having someone out there worrying about you, wanting to protect you. I could get used to that."

"Good. I'm really not good at playing the helpless female who stands on the sidelines wringing her hands."

Logan's heart tightened at the fleeting thought of Sarah. Scottie was headstrong, but she was smart where Sarah had been impulsive, a clear thinker even when her heart was engaged, where Sarah had let passion rule her actions. Logan realized in that moment just how little control he'd really had over Sarah's actions that night. Even had he not been involved with her, the chances of Sarah pulling a crazy stunt of some kind at some point were pretty high. Part of the responsibility would always be his, but he looked at Scottie and realized that for the first time, he could commit all of his heart with complete faith and trust.

"I'm not looking for a helpless female," he said quietly. "I'm looking for a partner. I'm looking for a woman who will stand for me and beside me, just as I will her. I'm looking for a woman who won't mind being watched over and won't mind watching over me as well. I'm looking for a woman I can champion no matter what life throws her way . . . and one who will champion me. I'm looking for my own dark knight."

"I'm not sure such a paragon of virtue exists." She spoke barely above a whisper.

"No paragon," he said. He felt her tremble in his arms. "Answer me this, Scottie, why is your field status compromised? Because you made love to me? To a man who was your assigned target?"

She shook her head slowly. "No. I lost my field status because I fell in love with the man I was assigned to protect, the man I made love to."

He thought his heart would burst wide open. He

never knew a person could feel such joy. "Then I guess I can stop looking."

He pulled her into his arms and kissed her deeply. "I love you, Anunsciata Bernadina."

"I love you, too, Logan Blackstone." She buried her head against his chest and held on tight.

"I only wish Blackie were still alive," Logan said. "He'd have loved you and vice versa."

"I can't give you that, but I can give you a brother that I know you'll love." She smiled. "He *is* the Lone Ranger. You guys can grow old swapping superhero stories. But we gotta rescue him and his lady love first." Her smile was sly as she winked up at him. "Shall we, James?"

Logan whooped and scooped her up in his arms, kissing her hard and long as he spun them both around. She was laughing and so was he as he set her feet back on the floor. His arms wrapped tightly around her, he grinned and said, "Absolutely, my dear Catwoman. Let's go save the planet one more time."

TWELVE

Scottie sat behind her desk in her office, observing the small crowd gathered there while she spoke into the phone. No one was paying attention to her. It was a New Year's celebration, albeit a few weeks late, and the atmosphere was festive.

She spun her chair around, facing away from the chatter, and looked out the floor-to-ceiling windows. A thick blanket of snow decorated downtown Denver. "Del, I was counting on you to be here today. You know how important it is to me for us to—" She broke off and listened to his protestations for a few seconds before breaking back in. "Blue is here. You owe this to your daughter, Seve. She should get the news from both of us. And don't chastise me for using her. I'm serious about getting you in here and not above using emotional blackmail to do it. Now, I plan to announce your return whether you want me to or not. If you want to have any control over how I do it, then I suggest you arrive in the next hour. And don't tell me you can't. I know you're in Denver. And if that's not enough, I have a feeling there might be another announcement made today that you'd like to hear as well." She hung up the phone without waiting for a reply.

She only hoped it worked.

"You going to come join the party, or don't they let the boss have a day off?"

Scottie smiled as she turned back to her desk. T. J. Delahaye, all six feet seven inches of the man, stood on the other side. "It's an ongoing compromise," she said. "That's why we're partying in my office." She looked around him. "Where's Jenna?"

"Talking to Blue and Diego. They hit it off right away. She's trying to talk them and the McShanes into coming out to the ranch." He looked pointedly at her.

She raised her hands, palms out. "I know, I know. I promised you I'd give you a date, and I will."

"He might be bigger, but nobody makes time with my woman without getting by me first." Logan stepped out from behind T.J. and skirted the desk.

His voice sent chills down her spine. His woman. Oh yes! She was still getting used to it, and she loved it. She laughed and looked up at him. "Hey, I can fight my own battles."

"What, and deprive us of some good testosterone-laden fun and adventure?" T.J. joked. He turned to Logan and extended a hand. "I don't think we've been formally introduced yet. T. J. Delahaye."

"Logan Blackstone," Logan responded, shaking his hand. "Although I guess that's not hard to figure out."

T.J. chuckled and looked across the room to Lucas, then back to Logan. "It is pretty wild seeing the two of you together. I'm glad it all worked out," he added sincerely.

Logan looked across the room, his chest tightening up as his gaze landed on his brother. Lucas looked up at that moment and the two shared a short smile and a nod. It was eerie, the instant connection he'd felt with Lucas, a complete stranger despite their genetic ties. They'd both talked about it many times over the last several weeks. "Yeah," he said, clearing his throat. "Me too."

Scottie tugged on his hand until Logan leaned over for a short kiss, delighting T.J., who made encouraging noises for her to continue. She blushed and broke it off, smiling private promises at Logan as he straightened. He fell in love with her all over again. Something he found he'd been doing on an almost hourly basis.

"I'm an incredibly lucky man," he said, looking into her eyes. "Very blessed."

T.J. said, "There's a lot of that sentiment floating around this room today. Hard to believe all the changes."

"You can say that again," Scottie said softly, still looking at Logan.

"I've been trying to get her to agree to come to the ranch and spend some time with me and Jenna. Maybe you can have some influence in that department." Just then a very tall, very striking woman made her way to T.J.'s side and ducked comfortably under his arm. Their size alone made them an arresting couple. But when T.J. looked down at Jenna and she smiled, Logan saw the true magic. He understood that magic.

"I've got Blue and Diego and John and Cali committed," Jenna said. She looked at Logan and Scottie. "How 'bout you two?"

"Honeymoon suite is open," T.J. said with an encouraging grin and a wink.

Jenna nudged her husband's shoulder. "Not everyone is as ready to race down the aisle as you were," she said.

"I recall it being a tie," T.J. reminded his wife, who could only smile and shrug.

"Well, you're welcome to come visit whenever you can make time," she said, smiling back at Scottie and Logan. "We'd love to have you."

John and Cali McShane walked up to the desk. "Good, are you talking her into taking a break?" John said. Handsome in a world-weary, Indiana Jones kind of way, he was one of the original Dirty Dozen. Scottie had also recruited his wife. They both worked on the internal side of the team now. "Give us a break from the slave driver," he added.

"Boy, I tell you, throw a party for your employees, and all you get is ragged on. Don't expect a big check in your bonus envelope this year."

Everyone rolled their eyes in a collective "get real" expression. She laughed. Money, while better than decent, was the least motivating factor for this crew.

Blue Santerra waltzed over and stood beside Scottie. "Don't let them box you in a corner, Scottie," she said, laying a hand on her shoulder. It was a measure of just how much she'd changed that Blue's hand felt comforting there. Blue had made a point of contacting Scottie when they'd come back from successfully completing their assignment in Montana. She'd been facing a dilemma and had needed Scottie's help. While they had talked, Scottie had actually opened up a bit herself and talked about her wildfire relationship with Logan. Blue had laughed and went on to explain how it had been similar for her and Diego. Blue was also a police officer with the Denver PD, and Scottie and she ended up talking shop as well.

The groundwork for a solid friendship had been laid that day, one that Scottie intended to work hard at nurturing. Blue had already made it clear that she wanted the four of them to spend time together. Scottie was looking forward to it. Logan and Diego in the same room would make for interesting conversation at the very least.

"Thanks, Blue. Always nice to have backup."

"Hey, it's my job." She laughed along with the rest of them.

Diego joined the cluster. "Did you tell them?" he asked quietly.

Blue looked at her husband and something in her posture seemed to melt. "Not yet. We should do that together." She turned to Scottie with a questioning look.

Scottie lifted a shoulder. "I did my best," she said for Blue's ears only. "All we can do is wait and see, I guess."

Blue nodded then turned to the group. "Okay guys, let's back up and give the new couple some breathing room here." She looked at a now wide-eyed Scottie and winked unapologetically. "Heavy breathing room."

Everyone laughed and little by little broke away into smaller clusters of talk and laughter.

Blue winked at Scottie and Logan again, then pulled her husband over to a quiet corner.

Scottie watched them go as Logan tugged her to stand. "I like her," Logan said.

"So do I," Scottie said, with true affection in her voice. "She's a good person. Diego is a lucky man."

Logan pulled her to his side and turned her face to his. "I'd say there are a whole bunch of very lucky people in this room. You have a good team, Commander. Good people."

"Thank you." Scottie knew Logan's full background now and took his comment as the respected compliment it was. He'd spent the past five years working for a deeply buried government task force whose job it was to pin down the globe's worst criminals. Terrorists and international arms dealers were Logan's specialty. "You still sure you want to do this?"

Logan kissed her deeply, reveling in the fact that she didn't pull away, that she didn't view public displays of affection as a weakness. Quite the opposite. "If you're talking about joining the team as an advisor on international threats, the answer is yes, I'm sure."

"And if I was talking about . . . something else?" She smiled softly when he kissed her gently on the lips, then blushed hotly when he whispered in her ear. He leaned away while he still could, but his devilish smile belied his casual tone. "Did you talk to Del?"

A frown creased her forehead as she nodded. "For all the good it did."

"Then he's not coming?"

She lifted a shoulder. "I don't know. I tried everything I could think of."

Logan grinned and squeezed her. "Then he'll be here. My woman always gets the job done."

Scottie's laughter was interrupted by the appearance

of Lucas. The resemblance still startled her, and when they stood side by side, the impact was almost visceral.

"Hi." In contrast to his brother, Lucas was a man of few words, generally remaining quiet. But Scottie knew that beneath his apparent shy exterior he was intensely alert, absorbing all the details around him without intruding on the scene. Scottie knew this was what made him so good at blending into any situation. She would miss him in the field. She'd tried to talk him into lending his expertise as a consultant, much as his brother was going to, but he'd shocked them all by announcing he was retiring from the profession altogether. He was going to head back to Michigan and take over Blackie's Place. In the end, it had been Logan who'd argued successfully in his brother's favor. Scottie lost the battle with grace. At least she liked to think she did. Logan still teased her about it.

"Hi, Lucas," she said. "I guess I should stop dominating your brother's attention here and let you two have some time alone together. When do you leave for Detroit?"

"Right after the holiday party for the kids," he said.

Scottie smiled softly. "I think that's the greatest idea you two had." All of the children from the Brethren compound, including several Scottie and Del hadn't known about, had been rescued. After returning to Denver, Logan and Lucas had put theirs heads together and decided to reunite the kids, now scattered with various extended family members, for a holiday party. For many of the children, it would be their first such celebration ever.

Lucas cleared his throat and looked at Logan for a second. He was clearly uncomfortable.

Scottie touched Lucas's arm—another change Logan had so quickly rendered in her life. Touching others came so naturally to her, she wondered how she'd stifled that part of her personality for so long. "Whatever it is, it can't be that bad. Just spit it out."

He looked her in the eye. "I'd like to host the reception for your wedding to Logan at Blackie's," he said all in one breath. "That is, once I get back there and get settled in." He looked at both of them. "You weren't planning on doing anything soon, were you?"

Truthfully, Scottie thought about marrying Logan at least every other minute of every day. All he had to do was nod at the closest justice of the peace, and she'd be there with bells on. Or a black catsuit. She stifled the private smile, not certain Lucas would understand. It was an odd feeling, realizing she knew Logan better than a man she'd worked with for a decade.

But though she knew Logan was her life and would be forever, and felt confident in his love for her, he hadn't actually popped the big question. She had already decided to take matters into her own hands, but this wasn't the way she wanted to do it. "We, uh, don't have any real concrete plans at this point."

"I didn't mean you had to marry there," Lucas added quickly, misreading the sudden tension. He turned to his brother. "I know Detroit doesn't hold the best of memories for you."

Scottie felt an emotion of an entirely different kind swamp her and tighten her throat as she watched the two brothers connect silently. Once Lucas had recovered from the shock of it all, their reunion had been highly emotional. She'd already told Logan that they would work something out for them to spend as much time together as possible. Family would be important to her, they would always know they came first. The team would have to adjust to her schedule.

To that end, she glanced at her watch again.

"I'm not sure what our plans are," Logan said, smoothing the tension away with his easy warmth. "But your offer means a lot to me." He glanced at Scottie. "To us. If we do anything, we'll do it with family. Thank you. And anytime you throw a party, call us, we'll be there." He leaned over and clapped Lucas on the shoulder, then grabbed his hand and raised it in a joint fist. "The Blackstone brothers return to Detroit! The city will never be the same."

Lucas grinned, making Scottie swallow. It made the most amazing change. The man was devastating when he smiled.

"Isn't he, though?" a female voice agreed from beside her.

Scottie turned to find Martina Gladiston standing beside her. She hadn't expected to like the woman, but Marti's personality was as short and sassy as her wild blond hair. She was a five-foot whirlwind. Scottie had ended up working behind the scenes to get a groundswell of excitement going over Marti's insider piece on cults. Marti had ended up wowing them on her own and had landed a five-part series with *The Washington Post*. *Newsweek* and *Time* were now vying to get her as a staff reporter.

Several television news shows had also been haunting her doorstep, but Marti was playing it straight and sticking with hard news over celebrity. She resolutely refused to discuss her father in any way and downplayed her instrumental role in rescuing the children. It had been Marti who'd discovered the additional children, all five of them infants. Scottie admired her as well as liked her.

Scottie smiled down at her. "Was I that obvious?"

Marti nodded, her flashy smile revealing perfect white teeth. "Yep." She sighed dramatically. "One of those smiles and I was a goner."

"I didn't know he was capable," Scottie said.

"Neither did he," Marti said, then laughed irrepressibly.

Lucas snagged her hand and tugged her to his side. "Hey there," he said quietly.

Marti smiled up at him and bumped his arm with her shoulder. "Hey there, yourself."

Scottie watched the byplay between them with unabashed interest. It was wonderful to see the quiet Blackstone brother try to hide his feelings. Especially when the other Blackstone brother made no attempt at all, much to her delight. And more to her delight, one kiss from Marti—a giant, noisy smacker of a kiss—and Lucas was forced to give up the pretense too.

Scottie squeezed Logan's hand and reached up for a kiss, seeing in his eyes the same warmth and delight over his newfound family as she had.

Logan and Lucas drifted into another one of their many conversations about the bar, and her thoughts turned back to Del. She was debating on whether to track him down and harass him again, when the double doors to her office swung open.

The silver-haired man that walked in was a complete stranger—to everyone in the room but her and Logan. She'd had her meeting with Del, several in fact, the last two of which Logan had sat in on. She was happy with the results, but she was thrilled that he'd decided to come there today. Only now did she really believe this was all going to work.

She walked over to him and took his hand. If he was surprised by the gesture, he masked it quickly. He held her gaze and then surprised her in return by stepping in and giving her a brief hug. "Thank you for bullying me into this," he said into her ear.

The buzz in the room quieted as people spied the latest guest, and then it quieted altogether when Scottie turned to face them.

"Everyone, I'd like to introduce you to your new co-commander."

"Daddy?" Blue's soft whisper traveled the entire length of the silent room. She pushed her way through the crowd until she stood before him.

Scottie watched as Del turned and focused his attention exclusively on his daughter. He nodded.

Blue looked him over. "Say something so I know it's you."

"It's me, *mi cielo.*"

My sky. The name he'd called her at birth, the name that had resulted in her being called Blue. "It is you," she said on a soft gasp. Her eyes grew glassy, and she threw her arms around him. "I thought you weren't coming back."

Del had been reunited with Blue, whom he hadn't seen since she was a child and who thought her father was dead, earlier that year, during the same assignment where she'd met Diego.

Blue broke the embrace and engulfed Scottie in a tight hug. "Thank you, Scottie. For bringing him back. Again."

"He was already back," Scottie said, returning the hug. "I just convinced him the world wouldn't come to an end if he stepped out of the shadows a little ways."

Del cleared his throat, obviously uncomfortable. Amid murmurs coming from the rest of the group, he said, "Shouldn't we get on with it?"

"Not yet," Blue interrupted. She turned and lifted her hand, signaling Diego. "There's another reason we wanted you here today." Diego came forward and tucked Blue to his side. They turned so they faced Del and the rest of the gathering. "I've been badgering Scottie for a month now, trying to get her to find me a way to contact you." Eyes shining at Scottie, she said, "This is so perfect." She looked back to Del. "You're going to be a grandfather, *mi padre*," she said with a soft smile.

Whoops and gasps followed by applause filled the office with cheerful noise. Suspicious moisture in his own eyes, Del stepped forward and pulled his daughter into a hug that was only awkward for a split second. Only when the applause had died down, leaving a few audible sniffles, did they pull apart.

Del laid his hand on his daughter's stomach. "I will make this child a promise." He looked into Blue's eyes. "I will be here for him or her. Always. Just as I will be here for you from now on."

Scottie wiped at the tears now flowing down her cheeks. Logan moved behind her and pulled her back against him in a comforting hug. He leaned down and whispered in her ear. "I want that to be our future, too, Anunsciata Bernadina. That *will* be us."

Scottie nodded, no longer trying to dry her eyes. She tipped her head back and looked up at Logan. "As long as you promise me that *I* get to name her if she's a girl."

Logan's mock wounded expression dissolved into chuckles.

Del cleared his throat and stepped toward the group. When the room was completely silent, he spoke.

"I started this team ten years ago at the request of our government. The guidelines I set for individual performance were strict and necessary if we were to succeed at the difficult assignments that Uncle Sam was going to ask of us. And we were successful. More than anyone could have hoped for. Every one of you can be proud of the work you've done, and under the most extreme circumstances and personal sacrifices." He paused for a moment and took time to look at each team member, new and old, individually.

"I haven't changed my stance on the requirements for a good field agent. But I have changed in other ways. I look at you, and I see some of the best agents I have ever had the pleasure to work with. I also look at you and see the beginnings of families." There was a collective holding of breath. "And I give you all my blessing."

Scottie squeezed Logan's hand and saw the other couples affirming their connections in their own personal way as well.

"It is time to move this team in a new direction. The Dirty Dozen as it existed has fulfilled its original mandate. Unfortunately there is still much work to be done. In order to do it most effectively, we will continue to firmly establish an internal base of operations and training as Scottie has already implemented."

"You're returning to the team?" This came from John McShane.

"Always the impatient one."

John simply smiled.

"An unrepentant lot," Del grumbled, but it was followed by a good-natured chuckle. "Went and fell in love despite yourselves." He bowed his head for a moment, as if composing himself, then looked up. "I consider it an honor to return to heading this team." He looked at Scottie. "I also consider it an honor to be brought into this growing family. There is a strength here that, though it is unfortunately a weakness in fieldwork, will be one of our biggest assets internally as the Dirty Dozen moves into the twenty-first century." He cleared his throat. "Thank you for forging ahead and proving to an old man that amidst chaos there can be love."

He raised his hands to fend off the sudden clamor of good wishes. "Scottie will brief you all later on the breakdown of command," he said gruffly, somewhat embarrassed by all the emotions running rampant in the room. "Essentially, she will continue to be in charge of setting up all ongoing training of current field agents. I will return to strategic command of our field operations." He looked at Blue. "I will be based here in Denver as well." He looked back to the group and said sharply, "So be prepared. I will be in these offices all the time. Look sharp, or you'll be hearing from me."

His attempt at stern command was an immediate failure as everyone moved forward and crowded around him, Blue, and Diego. Congratulations and welcomes were interspersed with hugs and backslaps.

Logan extricated Scottie from the throng and pulled her silently into the hall, easing the double doors shut behind him.

"Went pretty well, don't you think?" she asked.

"On a scale of one to ten, I think he hit about fifteen." He pulled her into his arms. "You did a good job, Scottie. Another mission successfully completed."

She smiled. One down. One to go. "He was so insistent on his input remaining anonymous, he really had me worried."

"He obviously had no idea who he was dealing with."

She held his approving gaze for a long, silent moment, drinking in the quiet strength he offered. "My dark knight, my champion in all things."

"Always."

"This is really going to work, isn't it?"

"Of course it is. All of it."

Scottie grinned back. "What a team. Nothing can stop us."

"Look out world, here comes the new dynamic duo." Logan kissed her. He released her suddenly. "I can't wait another second. I wanted to plan something really wonderful and romantic, but all those people in there so disgustingly happily married and—" He broke off and grinned. "Think you could handle being married to a superhero?"

"Could you?" she tossed back.

He swooped in and delivered a kiss that left her gasping and clinging to him. Of course, the way she'd kissed him back had rendered him the same. "Most definitely." He hugged her. "Most definitely." He pulled away enough to look at her. "But you have to promise me one thing. You'll wear the catsuit on our wedding night?"

She punched his shoulder even as she laughed. "See,

I knew you had latent latex fantasies. So, you want Catwoman, do you?" She snuggled up to him, purring, then ran a fingernail slowly down his chest. She continued to trail her nail down over the fly of his jeans.

He groaned. "Okay, no catsuit. You don't need one."

She looked him in the eye and smiled smugly. "You're right."

She beamed and pulled his head down for a long, deep kiss. When she had him reduced to gasping, she pulled away. "What are your plans for later this afternoon?"

"Plans?" His eyes were still glazed.

"Well, we do think alike. About those romantic plans . . . I had some of my own."

Logan grinned. "You were going to propose?"

"I have a room reserved at the Brown Palace for tonight. Would you care to join me?" She leaned in and delivered a growling purr next to his ear. "There might be latex involved."

"I'm there," he said weakly. Then he surprised a whoop of laughter out of her as he swung her up into his arms.

"Logan, put me—Where are you taking me?"

He strode down the hall toward the elevators.

"I have an office full of people. We can't leave right n—"

"We can. Del's there. He can take care of things. That's what delegating is all about."

"But—"

"When latex is involved, it's every man for himself." He kissed her silent as he stepped into the elevator. He didn't release her mouth until the doors opened in the parking garage. She wasn't arguing any longer. He grinned down into the face of the woman who had changed his life, who had given him back his life. The woman who was breathless and grinning back at him.

"So," he asked, walking on air, "do you think the Brown Palace has a chapel?"

She smiled slyly. "I know they do."

He chuckled. "I see another successful mission in your immediate future."

"I see a lifetime mission in my future."

Logan dropped her feet gently to the ground. "And we all know how important a successful mission is to you."

"Yeah," she said, going into his arms. "That we do." Tears sparkled in her eyes. "I can't promise you what kind of future we'll have, but I can promise you that you'll always come first. *We* will always come first."

"That's all I'll ever ask."

"I've given my whole life to my work, willingly. I'm proud of what I've accomplished and I'm looking forward to continuing, with you there fighting the good fight with me." She looked up into his eyes. "But I also want time for me. For us. I want time for family. I want to spend the rest of my life creating and building the family I always wanted and never had."

"We'll have all that and more, Scottie." He stepped closer. "In fact, that's a promise I intend to start keeping right now."

He pushed her back against the car and lowered his mouth to hers. Several moments later a throaty chuckle echoed through the empty garage. It was quickly followed by a low, whispered moan.

"Ohhhh, James."

THE EDITORS' CORNER

Since time began, women have struggled to be respected in the workplace. No longer damsels in distress, women have soared to the tops of their professions. Strength is measured in endurance, and with our own fifteenth anniversary coming this summer, we are celebrating strong women everywhere. Yet for all that our four heroines this month have accomplished, they learn that leaning on someone else for a change doesn't necessarily mean weakness. Relish these women in power and watch how their control crumbles in the wake of these fabulous heroes.

Helen Mittermeyer concludes her latest trilogy with the long-awaited **DESTINY SMITH**, LOVESWEPT #886, which is set once again in beautiful Yokapa County, New York. Helen visits with familiar friends and family as she reintroduces Destiny Smith and her soon-to-be-ex–husband Brace Coolidge.

When Brace refuses to sign the divorce papers and claims he wants to help adopt the two children Destiny has taken under her wing, she has no alternative but to come to an uneasy truce with the brash executive. With threats from all quarters hovering over their lives, Destiny and Brace struggle together to create a loving family for two children who have never known love. And in this struggle, can the two lovers find their way back to each other? Helen weaves a tale of turbulent emotion and sweet sensuality that brings together a rebel and the charming rogue who will try to tempt her into yielding her heart a second time around.

LOVESWEPT newcomer Caragh O'Brien presents her second release, **NORTH STAR RISING**, LOVESWEPT #887. Though river guide Amy Larkspur feels awkward in the bridesmaid dress she's wearing for her best friend's wedding, she doesn't show it when Josh Kita spies her on the balcony like a modern-day Juliet. The handsome widower knows that Amy's the *one*, whether he's ready for her or not. But with two young daughters to take care of, finding time to spend with Amy can get pretty hectic. Nevertheless, Josh pursues his beautiful dreamer with everything he's got. Amy can barely handle dealing with Josh, but add two children into the fold and she's definitely out of her league. Caragh O'Brien tries to solve the eternal puzzle of attraction in a novel as delightfully unpredictable as its spirited heroine.

In **JADE'S GAMBLE**, LOVESWEPT #888, Patricia Olney gives us Jade O'Donnell, single mother and co-owner of the Cinnamon Girl bakery, and Trace Banyon, sexy ex-fireman. Jade has had her share of marital strife—granted, it was only for half an hour, but it was enough heartache to last a lifetime. As a firefighter, Trace couldn't stop a mother and her son from dying, and in Jade and her son, Lucas, he sees his chance to atone for his past. Desperate to keep custody of Lucas, Jade is searching for a suitable candidate to be her husband. When Trace offers to step in, Jade decides that he's her only hope. United by a marriage of convenience, Jade and Trace soon learn that living as man and wife is a bigger gamble than they thought! Patricia Olney bakes up a savory romance to be tasted only by those who can handle happy endings.

Clint McCade teaches a few lessons in **BODY LANGUAGE** to chief executive officer Cassandra Kirk in Suzanne Brockmann's LOVESWEPT #889. World-renowned cameraman McCade has decided that his real home is with his best friend and true love, Sandy. The only problem is, she's in love with someone else. But like the pal that he is, McCade offers to help her get her man. Sandy is never surprised when McCade roars into town on the back of his Harley, but this time something's different. For one thing, McCade's never picked out her clothes or offered makeup advice before. And what is with those funny looks he keeps giving her, anyway? As the two begin a charade that becomes too hot for them to handle, they discover that the warm fuzzy feelings they have aren't just of friendship, but of love. Suzanne Brockmann proves her talent once again when she shows us the true meaning of best friends forever!

Happy reading!

With warmest wishes,

Susann Brailey   *Joy Abella*

Susann Brailey   Joy Abella

Senior Editor   Administrative Editor

P.S. Look for these women's fiction titles coming in May! Multiple-award-winning and bestselling author Deborah Smith enchants us with **A PLACE TO CALL HOME;** what the *Chicago Tribune* calls "a beautiful, believable love story" is now available in paperback. When Claire Delaney returns to her childhood home in Georgia to recuperate from an accident, she realizes that her love for Roan Sullivan has not diminished through the years. A turbulent reunion takes them to their childhood haunts and forces them to overcome twenty years of pain and separation in order to make a life together for themselves. Applauded by *Romantic Times* as "truly a bright light of the genre that shines brighter with each new novel," Karyn Monk returns with **THE WITCH AND THE WARRIOR,** a Scottish romance that ingeniously combines humor and passion. And immediately following this page, preview the Bantam women's fiction titles on sale in April!

For current information on Bantam's women's fiction, visit our Web site *Isn't It Romantic?* at the following address:
http://www.bdd.com/romance

Don't miss these exciting novels
from Bantam Books!

On sale in April:

WITH THIS RING
by Amanda Quick

A THIN DARK LINE
by Tami Hoag

NOBODY'S DARLING
by Teresa Medeiros

A HINT OF MISCHIEF
by Katie Rose

A THIN DARK LINE

by *New York Times* bestselling
author of *Guilty as Sin*

Tami Hoag

Available in paperback.

*Terror stalks the streets of Bayou Breaux, Louisiana.
A suspected murderer is free on a technicality, and
the cop accused of planting evidence against him is
ordered off the case. But Detective Nick Fourcade
refuses to walk away. He's stepped over the line before. This case threatens to push him over the edge.*

*He's not the only one. Deputy Annie Broussard
found the woman's mutilated body. She still hears
the phantom echoes of dying screams. She wants justice. But pursuing the investigation will mean forming an alliance with a man she doesn't trust and
making enemies of the men she works with. It will
mean being drawn into the confidence of a suspected
killer. For Annie Broussard, finding justice will
mean risking everything—including her life.*

*The search for the truth has begun—one that
will lead down a twisted trail through the steamy
bayous of Louisiana, and deep into the darkest
reaches of the human heart.*

Nationally bestselling author Teresa Medeiros
makes the American West her own in the new
completely captivating historical romance . . .

NOBODY'S DARLING
by Teresa Medeiros

*When pretty, young Bostonian Esmerelda Fine hears that
her brother has been killed out West, she sells everything
she owns and sets out to find her brother's murderer and
bring him to justice. But Billy Darling, the man accused of
the murder, is nothing like she expects. First of all, he's
devastatingly attractive. But second, not only does he claim
not to have killed her brother, it's beginning to look like
her brother is alive and well . . . a wanted man. When
Esmerelda hires Billy to track her brother down, the adventure, and the passion, have just begun. . . .*

Billy Darling was a jovial drunk.

Which explained the dangerous edge to his tem-
per as he surveyed the haughty young miss who had
presumed to interrupt his poker game. His first whiskey of the day sat untouched on the table just inches
from his fingertips. The way his day was going, he
doubted it would be his last.

The woman disagreed. Noting the direction of his
glance, she gave the brimming glass an imperious
nod. "You'd best finish your whiskey, sir. It may be
the last you taste for a very long while."

Billy barely resisted the urge to bust out laughing.
Instead, he curled his fingers around the glass and
lifted it in a salute to her audacity. She really ought to
be flattered by the stir her announcement had caused.

Noreen had gone tumbling off his lap in a flurry of scarlet petticoats while Dauber and Seal went diving under a nearby table, scattering bills and coins.

Only Drew had remained upright, but even he had scooted his chair back a good two feet and thrown his hands into the air. The waxed tips of his mustache quivered with alarm. Billy suspected he would have joined the cowboys under the table if he hadn't feared rumpling the new paisley waistcoat he'd had shipped all the way from Philadelphia. You could almost always count on Drew's vanity overruling his cowardice.

It wasn't the first time Billy had faced a woman across the barrel of a gun, and it probably wouldn't be the last. Hell, he'd even been shot once by a jealous whore in Abilene. But she'd cried so prettily and tended the wound and the rest of him with such gratifying remorse, he'd forgiven her before the bleeding stopped.

It wasn't even that he particularly minded being shot by a woman. He just wanted to do something to deserve it first.

He drained the rest of the whiskey in a single searing swallow and thumped the glass to the table, making her flinch. "Why don't you put the gun down? You really don't want to get powder burns on your pretty white gloves, do you, Miss . . . ?"

"Fine. Miss Esmerelda Fine."

She flung her name at him like a challenge, but it failed to trigger even an echo of recognition. "Esmerelda? Now that's a rather lofty name for such a little bit of a lady. Suppose I just call you Esme?"

He would have thought it impossible, but her mouth grew even more pinched. "I'd rather you didn't. My brother was the only one who called me Esme." Then that same mouth surprised him by curving into a sweetly mocking smile. "Unless, of course, you'd rather I call you *Darling*?"

Billy scowled at her. "The last man who cast aspersions on my family name got a belly full of lead." In reality, he'd only gotten a bloody nose, but since Billy didn't plan to give either to this persistent young lady, he didn't see any harm in embellishing.

"It wouldn't have been my brother, by any chance, would it? Is that why you gunned down a defenseless boy? For hurting your poor, delicate feelings?"

"Ah." Billy's good humor returned as he folded his arms over his chest and tilted his chair back on two legs. "Now we're getting somewhere. Do refresh my memory, Miss Fine. You can't expect me to remember every man I'm supposed to have killed."

"I should have expected no less than such callous disregard from an animal like you, Mr. Darling. A cold-blooded assassin masquerading as a legitimate bounty hunter." Her contemptuous gaze flicked to Drew. "Sheriff, I demand that you arrest this man immediately for the murder of Bartholomew Fine III."

"What happend to the first two Bartholomews?" Dauber whispered. "Billy kill them, too?"

Seal elbowed him in the ribs, earning a sharp grunt.

Drew twirled one tip of his mustache, a habit he indulged in only in moments of great duress. "Now, lass," he purred in that lilting mixture of Scottish burr and western drawl that was so exclusively his. "There's no reason to get your wee feathers all in a ruffle. I remain confident that this private quarrel between you and Mr. Darling can be settled in a civilized manner without the discharge of firearms."

"Private quarrel?" The woman's voice rose to a near shriek. "According to that Wanted poster out there, this man is a public menace with a price on his head. I insist that you take him in!"

Drew sputtered an ineffectual retort, but Billy's melted-butter-and-molasses drawl cut right through it. "And just where do you propose he take me?"

Miss Fine blinked, her face going blank for a gratifying moment. "Why, the jail, I suppose."

Billy slanted Drew a woeful look. Avoiding Miss Fine's eyes, Drew polished his badge with his ruffled shirtsleeve. "Sorry, lass, but our jail's not equipped to hold Mr. Darling. You'll have to take your complaint to the U.S. marshal in Santa Fe."

Righting his chair, Billy favored her with a rueful grin, briefly entertaining the notion that she and her sad little bonnet just might admit defeat and creep away to let him finish his poker game in peace. After all, any fellow hapless enough to be stuck with the name of Bartholomew was probably better off dead.

She dashed his hopes by swaying forward, her voice husky with menace. "If this miserable excuse for a lawman—"

"Now wait just one minute there, lass!" Drew cried, his Scottish accent deepening along with his agitation. If she got him any more riled, there would be *g*'s dropping and *r*'s rolling all over the saloon. "There's no need to insult my—"

She turned the gun on him; his defense subsided to a sulky pout. She returned it to Billy, aiming it square at his heart.

"If this miserable excuse for a lawman won't take you in," she repeated firmly, "then I will. I'll take you to Santa Fe and turn you over to the U.S. marshal myself. Why, I'll hog-tie you to the back of a stagecoach and drag you all the way to Boston if I have to, Mr. Darling."

Billy sighed wearily. She'd left him with no choice but to call her bluff. As the smile faded from his eyes, the bartender vanished behind the bar, Drew inched his chair backward, and Dauber and Seal plugged their ears with their fingertips.

Billy rested his hands palms-down on the table, flexing his fingers with deceptive indolence. "Oh, yeah?" he drawled. "Who says?"

Little Miss Fine-and-Mighty cocked the derringer, her face going white with strain. "I've got one shot in this chamber that says you're coming with me."

The Colt .45 appeared in Billy's hand as if by magic, accompanied by a personable grin. "And I've got six shots in this here Colt that say I'm not."

Esmerelda stared dumbly at the gun in Darling's hand. His movements hadn't betrayed even a hint of a blur. One second his hand had been empty. The next it had been cradling an enormous black pistol. The imposing barrel dwarfed the stunted mouth of her derringer, making it look like a toy. Darling's smile was unflinching, but all traces of green had disappeared from his eyes, leaving them ruthless chips of flint.

Esmerelda sucked in a steadying breath, cringing when it caught in a squeak. She'd spent so many sleepless nights in the past few months dreaming of the moment when she would confront her brother's murderer. But none of the possible scenarios had included engaging him in a standoff. Billy Darling was rumored to be a crack shot, lethally accurate at thirty yards, much less four feet. What was the proper etiquette in these situations? Should she suggest they choose seconds? Step outside and draw at twenty paces? She flexed her numb fingers, choking back a hysterical giggle.

Almost as if he'd read her mind, he said, "It has occurred to me, Miss Fine, that this may very well be your first gunfight. We have both drawn our weapons so all that remains is to determine which one of us has the guts to pull the trigger. If you'd rather not find out, then I suggest you lay your gun on the table and back out of here. Nice and slow."

"Now, William," the sheriff whined. "You know you've never shot a woman before."

Darling's affable smile did not waver. "Nor has one ever given me cause to."

"Drop your weapon, sir," Esmerelda commanded, praying the derringer wouldn't slip out of her sweat-dampened glove. She waited a respectable interval before adding a timid,

"P-p-please."

"I asked you first."

She'd forfeited all she held dear just to come to this godforsaken town and bring her brother's killer to justice. And there he sat, smirking at her with cool aplomb, all the while knowing that he had crushed her brother's life beneath his boot heel with no more concern than for a discarded cigar butt.

Esmerelda suddenly realized that she no longer wanted justice. She wanted vengeance. Her finger tightened on the trigger. A scalding tear trickled down her cheek, then another. She dashed them away with one hand, but fresh ones sprang into their place to blur her vision.

She did not see the sheriff rock back in his chair, grinning with relief. Billy Darling might be able to stand down the meanest desperado in five territories or gun down a fleeing outlaw without blinking an eye, but he never could abide a woman's tears.

"Aw, hell, honey, don't cry. I didn't mean to scare you. . . ."

Billy was out of his seat and halfway around the table, hand outstretched, when Esmerelda Fine, who had never so much as swatted a fly without a pang of regret, closed her eyes and squeezed the trigger.

"Fresh, charming, warm and witty, Katie Rose
writes deliciously romantic stories.
I can't wait to read more of them!"
—Teresa Medeiros, nationally bestselling author

From a delightful new voice comes a totally unique
historical romance: a clever and utterly irresistible
tale of New York City in the "Age of Innocence,"
where a lady who talks to spirits discovers just how
heavenly passion can be when you add . . .

A HINT OF MISCHIEF
by Katie Rose

*For the bewitching Jennifer Appleton and her charming
sisters, there is nothing the least bit wicked about holding a
séance. The spirits the trio conjure up seem to offer the
unhappy matrons of Victorian Manhattan a great deal of
comfort . . . and after all, impoverished young ladies
have to make a living somehow. So it's something of a
shock when a darkly handsome and coldly furious stranger
shows up at their door, aiming accusations of fraud—and
his remarkably compelling gaze—at lovely, wide-eyed Jennifer.*

*Convinced she's swindled his grieving mother out of a
sizable sum, Gabriel Forester swears he'll put this brazen
conniver out of business for good. But the lady he confronts
is a total revelation—and a surprising temptation. Now, as
the fiery opponents square off, passion flares unexpectedly,
and Gabriel and Jennifer find themselves drawn into a
devilish game of seduction where they must learn to ignore*

the ghostly voices of the past . . . and listen to their hearts.

It was her. The devil herself, Jennifer Appleton. She was dressed in a pretty dotted-white-on-white Swiss chiffon, a pink sash tied just below her breasts. The dress was a little old-fashioned, but of good material and lovely styling. He had difficulty pulling his eyes away from her, for as he had supposed, her figure was magnificent. It was generously exposed by the light quality of her dress, and he surmised she wore little beneath the gown. Although the heat made such considerations practical, it was scandalous nevertheless.

When she finally lifted her face, he saw that she bloomed with color. If the fright of the lawyer's letter affected her, it was not apparent in her easy manner, her full, lush giggles, nor her joie de vivre as she swung a croquet mallet and deftly landed her ball just outside the wicket. She must have felt his observation, for her eyes met his and held him spellbound.

"Jennifer! You must come! Oh please, they are asking for you!"

A beautiful woman approached her, and Gabriel identified Jennifer's sister. Penelope led her away to a group of women clustered beneath a shade tree with their ices and fans. Gabriel recognized Mesdames Merriweather and Greyson, the Misses Billings and Miss Barry. He waited for their rebuff, but instead, they seemed genuinely pleased to meet 'The Appleton.' Their talk grew animated, and Gabriel drifted close enough to hear the conversation.

"Is it true that you brought Mary Forester's husband back from the dead? What was it like?" Eleanore Greyson asked, her stern face lit up with excitement.

"How do you do it? Can you feel the ghostly presence?" The normally reserved Margaret Merri-weather questioned.

"Are you frightened, living alone, knowing that spirits have been in your house?" Jane Billings wanted to know, her voice pleading.

"How do you give such marvelous readings? I've heard of your powers from several sources!" Judith Barry gushed.

Stunned, Gabriel saw Jennifer wield her power like a queen deigning to speak with peasants. She answered their questions cleverly, making them curious for more. Idly he realized her intelligence outweighed her beauty, but more obvious was her formidable charm. That, Jennifer Appleton had in boatloads.

Incensed, Gabriel was about to accost her when Jonathan Wiseley stole up beside him, a glass of beer in one hand, a chocolate cake in the other. "Pretty girl," he remarked, chomping on the cake. "I hear she's taking New York by storm."

"What are you talking about?" Gabriel blazed, and the young man nearly choked on his beer.

"Well, didn't you know? The 'bewitching trio' has been seen everywhere. They had tea at the Billingses, lunch at the Swathmores. I hear they've been invited to every major outing this summer. No one seems to know much about them, except that their parents, who were of good family, died. Poor dears! But there's no doubt as to their success."

Gabriel saw the truth of the man's words as the women piled knee-deep to get a word with Jennifer. Far from being out of her element, she played the crowd like a conductor of an orchestra. Worse, she seemed to be enjoying herself immensely, for she fanned herself prettily, letting the heat climb in her cheeks. Soon men surrounded her, and Gabriel could hear them fighting over who would bring her a glass of punch.

"As I said, poor little orphans. I for one would certainly like to adopt one of them. Say, do you think they are free lovers like that creature Woodhull? That would be terribly convenient, wouldn't it?"

Gabriel opened his mouth to retort, but didn't trust himself to speak. For some reason, he was furious with Jonathan's comment, and even more furious with the men thronging around Jennifer. Turning rudely away from Jonathan, he approached her, and heard her trying to decide whether to attend the Adam's ball, or the Chambers Street festival, a decision she seemed to enjoy mightily.

"Miss Appleton, I beg a private word with you." Gabriel sent her a look that brooked no refusal. As the men booed, Jennifer shrugged her dainty white shoulders, then descended from the crowd. Gabriel took her by the arm and practically dragged her into the rose garden.

"Unhand me this minute!" Jennifer cried as soon as they were alone.

Gabriel released her, suddenly aware that he *was* still holding her arm. Jennifer Appleton stood in front of him amid the Barrymores' prized Silver Lace roses, looking incredibly beautiful. Instead of appearing frightened by his confrontation, she held her chin up defiantly, as if prepared to defend her ground at all costs.

She looked so adorable Gabriel had trouble staying angry. He had to remind himself of exactly who she was—and what she was. "Miss Appleton," he managed sternly, "what are you doing here? Is it common for tea-leaf readers, who bilk elderly ladies out of money, to entertain at garden parties in such a manner?"

"And what, sir, is your objection?"

He could have sworn he saw laughter lurking at the corners of her mouth. He gestured to her gown.

"I think you know exactly what I mean. That you are here, dressed like that, flaunting yourself before the men! How did you get invited to this gathering, or did you just crash the gates?"

She was so close, he could smell her lilac water, so reminiscent of the letter to Charles. She was even prettier here than at a distance, for she seemed to emanate an energy and vitality that was intoxicating. His own thoughts drove him to distraction. Part of him wanted to put her over his knee and beat some sense into her; the other part wanted to kiss her until she swooned.

"I was invited by Madame Barrymore herself, thanks to a recommendation by the Misses Billings," Jennifer said indignantly, although she didn't seem entirely displeased with the situation. "As to my dress, it is no different than Sally Vesper's gown, nor Marybeth's. And I wasn't flaunting myself; I find the company of this society very congenial. I also find *your* interest questionable, since you are here escorting a female."

He gaped at her, outraged that she should turn his questions back on him. "You are the most exasperating woman I've ever had the misfortune to meet! Do you know what they are saying about you? They think you are like Victoria Woodhull, a free lover as well as a spiritualist! Is that the reputation you want?"

"I see." She lowered her face, appearing appropriately demure, but Gabriel knew better. He could almost sense her restrained mirth. When she looked up a moment later, it was as if a halo encircled her fair head.

"I truly appreciate your concern. As a gentleman, it was most kind of you to instruct me in the error of my ways. I am reformed, sir, thanks to you. I shall be forever grateful."

With that, she rose on her pink slippers and

placed a schoolmistress-like peck on his cheek. "Good day, Mr. Forester. I leave you the garden."

Gabriel's admiration mingled with his outrage and disbelief as Jennifer daintily curtsied, then swirled to walk gracefully out of the glade. Evidently, she saw him as some mawkish schoolboy she could toy with. His thoughts went back to her legal reply to Charles's letter, to the incident with the police, even to his first confrontation with her. So far, she had bested him at every turn. He had to appreciate her audacity, even as it enraged his male ego. She badly needed a lesson, Gabriel decided. One that he would teach her.

"Miss Appleton?"

He laid his hand on her shoulder, intending to give her a well-deserved dressing down, but she turned so quickly that she wound up in his arms. The merriment disappeared from her eyes and she looked at him with something else, something that made him think she didn't entirely despise him back. His chastising words suddenly caught in his throat as he gazed into her eyes, eyes that had convinced lesser souls they'd seen a ghost. As if of its own accord, his mouth lowered to hers, unable to resist the soft, sweet temptation.

On sale in May:

*A PLACE TO
CALL HOME*
by Deborah Smith

*THE WITCH AND
THE WARRIOR*
by Karyn Monk

Bestselling Historical Women's Fiction

❋ AMANDA QUICK ❋

____28354-5 SEDUCTION ...$6.50/$8.99 Canada

____28932-2 SCANDAL ....$6.50/$8.99

____28594-7 SURRENDER ....$6.50/$8.99

____29325-7 RENDEZVOUS ....$6.50/$8.99

____29315-X RECKLESS ....$6.50/$8.99

____29316-8 RAVISHED ....$6.50/$8.99

____29317-6 DANGEROUS ....$6.50/$8.99

____56506-0 DECEPTION ....$6.50/$8.99

____56153-7 DESIRE ....$6.50/$8.99

____56940-6 MISTRESS ....$6.50/$8.99

____57159-1 MYSTIQUE ....$6.50/$7.99

____57190-7 MISCHIEF ....$6.50/$8.99

____57407-8 AFFAIR ....$6.99/$8.99

❋ IRIS JOHANSEN ❋

____29871-2 LAST BRIDGE HOME ...$5.50/$7.50

____29604-3 THE GOLDEN

BARBARIAN ....$6.99/$8.99

____29244-7 REAP THE WIND ......$5.99/$7.50

____29032-0 STORM WINDS ....$6.99/$8.99

Bestselling Historical Women's Fiction

⚜ IRIS JOHANSEN ⚜

____28855-5 THE WIND DANCER ...$5.99/$6.99

____29968-9 THE TIGER PRINCE ...$6.99/$8.99

____29944-1 THE MAGNIFICENT

ROGUE ....$6.99/$8.99

____29945-X BELOVED SCOUNDREL .$6.99/$8.99

____29946-8 MIDNIGHT WARRIOR ..$6.99/$8.99

____29947-6 DARK RIDER ....$6.99/$8.99

____56990-2 LION'S BRIDE ....$6.99/$8.99

____56991-0 THE UGLY DUCKLING... $5.99/$7.99

____57181-8 LONG AFTER MIDNIGHT.$6.99/$8.99

____10616-3 AND THEN YOU DIE.... $22.95/$29.95

⚜ TERESA MEDEIROS ⚜

____29407-5 HEATHER AND VELVET .$5.99/$7.50

____29409-1 ONCE AN ANGEL ......$5.99/$7.99

____29408-3 A WHISPER OF ROSES .$5.99/$7.99

____56332-7 THIEF OF HEARTS ....$5.50/$6.99

____56333-5 FAIREST OF THEM ALL .$5.99/$7.50

____56334-3 BREATH OF MAGIC ...$5.99/$7.99

____57623-2 SHADOWS AND LACE ...$5.99/$7.99

____57500-7 TOUCH OF

ENCHANTMENT.........$5.99/$7.99

Ask for these books at your local bookstore or use this page to order.

Please send me the books I have checked above. I am enclosing $____ (add $2.50 to cover postage and handling). Send check or money order, no cash or C.O.D.'s, please.

Name _____

Address _____

City/State/Zip _____

Send order to: Bantam Books, Dept. FN 16, 2451 S. Wolf Rd., Des Plaines, IL 60018
Allow four to six weeks for delivery.
Prices and availability subject to change without notice.   FN 16 3/98